"I never dreamed I'd feel like this again."

Leo drew Davina down to sit on the bed beside him as he spoke. "Davy, I want you to share my life. But I'm years older than you. You ought to be thinking of marriage with some young, enthusiastic chap with less mileage to his credit."

"I'm not buying a secondhand car!" she replied forcefully. "And right now I don't want to marry anyone very much—not even you."

Davina didn't want Leo to go away and leave her alone. And neither did she want him with his mind even faintly preoccupied with regrets for a lost love. "Couldn't we just stay the way we are, Leo?"

"Friends, you mean?" Leo's voice was almost inaudible.

"No. I thought we could be more than that."

"Lovers?"

"Yes. Please."

Catherine George was born in Wales, and following her marriage to an engineer, lived for eight years in Brazil at a gold mine site, an experience she would later draw upon for her books. It was not until she and her husband returned to England and bought a village post office and general store that she submitted her first book at her husband's encouragement. Now her husband helps manage their household so that Catherine can devote more time to her writing. They have two children, a daughter and a son, who share their mother's love of language and writing.

Books by Catherine George

HARLEQUIN ROMANCE

2535—RELUCTANT PARAGON
2571—DREAM OF MIDSUMMER
2720—DESIRABLE PROPERTY
2822—THE FOLLY OF LOVING
2924—MAN OF IRON

HARLEQUIN PRESENTS

640—GILDED CAGE
698—IMPERFECT CHAPERONE
722—DEVIL WITHIN
800—PRODIGAL SISTER
858—INNOCENT PAWN
873—SILENT CRESCENDO
992—THE MARRIAGE BED
1016—LOVE LIES SLEEPING
1065—TOUCH ME IN THE MORNING

This Time Round

Catherine George

Harlequin Books

TORONTO • NEW YORK • LONDON
AMSTERDAM • PARIS • SYDNEY • HAMBURG
STOCKHOLM • ATHENS • TOKYO • MILAN

Original hardcover edition published in 1988
by Mills & Boon Limited

ISBN 0-373-02942-X

Harlequin Romance first edition November 1988

CHAPTER ONE

AT TEN minutes past seven on the evening of her seventeenth birthday Davina Lennox fell in love for the first time. Not a soul noticed. The Lennox household, not famous for tranquillity at any time, was in festive uproar for her birthday dinner, and the noise in the entrance hall, which doubled as dining-room for special occasions, was deafening due to the heated political argument raging between her father and brothers, and augmented by stringent comments from Mrs Lennox and her son's wives, Hetty and Sarah, as they helped her set the table with the best china and crystal, and lit candles in the silver candelabra that were Mrs Lennox's pride and joy.

Ever after Davina could conjure up the scene at will, indelible and vivid in her mind's eye; her father in the act of opening the wine, Ben and Joe laughing with their wives as the girls manoeuvred the heated trolley through the door from the kitchen, Mrs Lennox frowning anxiously at the clock. Davina herself, excused for the occasion from all chores, had tucked herself well away on the settle under the stairwell. She was listening idly to the others as she fondled the ears of Casey, the Irish wolfhound, when the knock thundered on the door. Mrs Lennox beamed and flew to let in her youngest son Sean, her welcome in no way diminished when exuberant, black-haired Sean simultaneously hugged his mother and presented her with an extra guest for dinner. Unexpected guests never troubled Mrs Lennox. She was used to them. And on that momentous night, with all Davina's favourite dishes provided in abundance for the birthday feast, an extra mouth to feed was even less of a problem than usual.

'Remember Leo Seymour? Old mate of mine from college.' Sean ushered his companion into the brightly lit hall and banged the door shut on the chill November night. 'I nipped into the Crown for a quick one on the way, and found Leo there.' He grinned at his mother. 'Couldn't abandon him to the Crown cuisine when I knew what would be on offer here tonight!'

All the Lennox family, bar one, took pains to make the unexpected guest welcome, brushing aside his well-bred apologies for intrusion on a family party. Davina, forgotten in her corner, looked on the face of Leo Seymour, and was lost. It was a narrow, bony face under unruly, tawny-red hair, with dark eyes that laughed at the world from under half-closed lids, and he was tall and whip-thin, yet wonderfully elegant, she thought worshipfully, even in casual sweater and jeans. He gestured at the latter, his face rueful as he eyed the festive board, and abruptly Davina became conscious of the spot on her chin, of the extra pounds she was always meaning to diet away, of the dress that had seemed so right in the shop and now, for some reason, was so horribly wrong. She eyed Hetty's bronze curls, Sarah's narrow hips, and burned with unfamiliar envy as she touched a despairing hand to ' her own untidy mop—striped in every shade from flax to mouse, and badly in need of the trim her mother had been nagging about for weeks. Casey rubbed his head against her knee in sympathy, and Davina was seized with a wild longing for escape, unable to cope with this unfamiliar feeling that dried her mouth and made her heart bang against her ribs. She yearned to slip away with the willing Casey and leave them all to it, but Nemesis, in the shape of Margaret Lennox, soon put a stop to that.

'Come along, Davina.' She held out a peremptory hand. 'Mr Seymour, we're forgetting our birthday girl—the baby of the family.'

Davina, who in the normal way of things enjoyed a warm, loving relationship with her mother, glared at her parent as she was absorbed, unwilling, into the circle surrounding Leo Seymour.

Sean gave her a bear-hug and handed her a bulky parcel wrapped in golliwog-printed paper. 'Happy birthday, Davy! Come and meet Leo Seymour.'

Hot with embarrassment, choked with suppressed emotion, Davina put out a hand in response to the strong, slim one extended to her, and muttered, 'How do you do,' without looking up into Leo Seymour's eyes, certain that the laughter in them must be at her own expense. To her utter confusion he bent towards her and kissed her cheek as he wished her happy birthday, and she leapt away as if his mouth had scalded her, muttering something unintelligible about helping with the meal as she darted away to the kitchen, which earned a scolding from her mother on lack of manners as they swiftly divided the prawn mousse into nine portions instead of eight.

Could she really have been so naïve—so bird-brained? Davina felt a century older than her teenage self, not a mere six or seven years. She eyed the blurred newspaper photograph as she drank her coffee, irritated that the sight of Leo Seymour's face, even of his name in print, still had the power to affect her, after all this time.

'Controversial director Leo Seymour en route to undisclosed location of latest film', said the caption. Davina pushed the paper away and cleared the table of her frugal breakfast, then coaxed Casey out into the garden for a walk before she left for the day. It was very early, but already the June day was warm and tantalisingly beautiful, and she wandered through the garden with the dog loping beside her, feeling restless and unusually disinclined for her day's work at the medical centre in the village.

Damn the man! Why couldn't he have done something more worthy and anonymous for a living, something totally uninteresting to the media?

Davina sat down, staring blindly at the garden. It would, of course, be impossible to block him out of her life altogether. Since her darling brother Sean had seen fit to run off with the love of Leo's life, it was a little tricky trying to pretend the wretched man didn't exist. God, what a mess it had all been. The mere thought of it still had the power to make her shudder, her animosity towards Sean to flare up right on cue, while her feelings towards Madeleine, his wife . . .

Casey pushed his head under Davina's arm and she stroked him absently, her mind going back inevitably to the evening of her birthday dinner, and how much she had enjoyed listening to Leo, who was, as he put it, assistant to the assistant producer of a film being made at Hadfield Chase, a half-ruined old house in the area. She had listened, rapt, as he told them about the film, which was on the subject of Lord Byron's scandalous relationship with his half-sister Augusta Leigh, with the handsome young Welsh actor John Wynne Jones cast as the poet and Madeleine Deane, highly promising new actress, as Augusta.

The entire Lennox clan had been utterly fascinated by Leo's account of the film as they ate, Sean teasing his friend over the incestuous theme, but to Davina the crowning miracle of the evening had been when Leo offered to take her over to Hadfield Chase for the day the following weekend. Head over heels in love, the young Davina had trotted after Leo Seymour on the day out like a devoted puppy, lost in bliss at the thought of how different he was from the pop-stars and footballers her friend Candida Mason mooned over. Leo Seymour was clever and witty and kind and—and glamorous. He actually worked in films! Who, of her schoolgirl contemporaries, could come up with anyone to top that?

Silly little idiot! Davina jumped up abruptly and went into the house, her mood thoroughly bad-tempered as she showered and dressed in readiness for her day.

It had all been so unbearable at the time. Madeleine had been so scared of Leo's reaction that she went into hiding, refusing to allow Leo to be told where she was, and Davina had had to lie to him, hating every moment, terrified by the wild look in his eyes as he questioned her. Mr and Mrs Lennox's censure of Sean and his fiancée had been bitter, and as soon as he found somewhere to go Sean had taken the guilt-ridden, lovesick girl off to London. Davina smiled wryly at the memory of how helpless Madeleine had been before the force of her sudden, overwhelming passion for Sean, then she sobered as she remembered Leo's anguish. Since she was witness to it all, their common experience had been enough to prevent Davina Lennox from ever laying herself open to the hurt that seemed synonymous with falling in love. Once bitten was twice shy as far as she was concerned. Her life was very satisfactory as it was. Plenty of boyfriends, but no lovers.

But you thought Leo was the greatest thing on two legs, a mental voice reminded her. You worshipped him. Admit it. God, how she had agonised over his torment, spending sleepless nights trying to think of ways to comfort him, wishing that, anguish though they were for him, Leo's frustrated passions were expended on herself rather than Madeleine. How shyly she had fantasised over situations where she smoothed his hair away from his fevered brow and he looked at her with new eyes, realising her worth, her quality, how superior she was to Madeleine in every way barring her lack of years. In her dream he turned to her and drew her close, kissing her gently on the lips as he had done at the end of their beautiful, golden day together at Hadfield Chase.

'Help me forget Madeleine,' the dream-Leo had breathed, and fervently she had promised him she would.

Straight out of the egg, thought Davina as she skirted the village duck-pond and smiled at the postman. What a dimwit she had been—more like seven than seventeen.

Somehow it had all seemed so much worse because she had known that underneath it all the real Leo wasn't like that in the least. It was the jealousy burning in him like acid which was the real culprit, distorting his personality to the point where he had no regard for the hurt he was inflicting on Davina in his obsession with Madeleine's whereabouts. Leo had driven her frantic with constant merciless interrogation, but at least she had seen him, been with him for a little. Even though she was witness to his unhappiness, it had been worth it just to be in his company. She tried to be philosophical, telling herself that if nothing else the whole sorry business had taught her a useful lesson about the pitfalls of falling in love. At first hand she had witnessed the utter ruthlessness of both Sean and Leo in the throes of their common passion, Sean's total disregard of his friend's feelings in his own urge to possess Madeleine, Leo careless of Davina's in his rough-riding efforts to wring the truth out of her. All in all it had been very off-putting.

'You mustn't let all this business upset you so much, darling,' Margaret Lennox had told her. 'None of it was your fault, Davina. Try to forget it.'

Easier said than done. Of course it was gratifying to find that eight or nine pounds of puppy-fat had departed with her appetite, which made her cheekbones more prominent and her eyes bigger, and gave her looks a hint of fragility Davina knew was not imaginary, since even her father passed comment on it. Both her parents gave voice to their misgivings about her too much for Davina's liking, and she was heartily glad on that evening when they went off for their weekly bridge game and left her alone with Casey. She was huddled on the hearthrug in front of the fire, wielding a brush on hair still damp from her bath, when the doorbell rang. Casey leapt up, barking, and Davina followed suit more cautiously, tightening the sash of her father's old red silk dressing-gown before going to the door. She opened it a crack, then would have banged it shut again except that Leo's booted foot shot out to prevent her. 'Please, Davy,' he said urgently. 'I'd like a word with your father.'

Davina stared at him suspiciously, the wind taken out of her sails. Leo looked haggard, it was true, and his eyes were bloodshot from lack of sleep, but he seemed relatively calm. With a sigh she opened the door.

'Oh, very well, you can come in if you like, but there's nobody here but me—and Casey.' She let go of the dog's collar and Casey flew at Leo, but only to fawn over him, and Leo gentled the animal, standing where he was in the open doorway, his eyes turning instinctively towards the stairs. She followed his look with scorn. 'It's the truth, Leo. My parents are out playing bridge and I'm reading some Hardy for an essay, Casey here is keeping me company, and that's it. Sum total of the Lennox household. So either go away or come in and shut the door. I'm freezing.'

Leo's face was expressionless as he closed the door behind him. Davina felt uneasy as he stood looking at her in silence. It was an effort not to shift from one foot to the other under the scrutiny of his unsmiling dark eyes.

'I came to apologise,' he said at last.

'Apologise? To my father?'

'No. To you. But at the same I intended to talk with your father. Appeal to his sense of justice.' He smiled with irony. 'Since Mr Lennox is a solicitor, I assumed he'd try to see my point of view.'

'Oh, he does. Both he and Mother are in full sympathy with you, Leo, believe me.' Davina hesitated, then motioned him towards the sitting-room. 'Come in and sit down if you like. You can wait for them to get home as long as you don't start on me again about—about your obsession.' She gestured upwards as they passed the stairs. 'Perhaps you'd like to make a quick tour of inspection first—see for yourself that the house is empty. Go in any room you want; I don't mind. Only mine's a mess.'

Leo shook his head, something very like shame on his face as he held open the door for her. 'You make me feel very small, Davy. There's no excuse for the way I've behaved to you these past few days, I know. I've been off my head with—with——'

'Jealousy. And I was the only one you could take it out on.' Davina gave him a very disillusioned little smile. 'What you wanted was to knock Sean's teeth down his throat, then make violent love to Madeleine, I suppose, whereas the only relief you could get was by hounding me.'

Leo slumped down on the sofa, his head in his hands, as Davina resumed her former place on the rug. 'You have every right to make me feel like a worm,' he said quietly. 'You can't possibly despise me any more than I despise myself. And today I reached a new low.'

Davina looked up at him quickly. 'What happened?'

'Because Madeleine's taken off and there's some problem with censorship. The backer's withdrawn. The film's been cancelled.'

'Oh, Leo, I'm so sorry,' said Davina, stricken. 'Really I am. I only wish there was something I could do.'

'Not your fault, little one. You can't answer for Sean's sins.'

'Madeleine's too!'

Leo's head went up, his eyes kindling, then he

shrugged. 'Anyway, this is the last time I'll trouble you. I'm off tomorrow.'

'What will you do?'

'God knows. At the moment I don't care very much.'

'Oh, for heaven's sake stop being such an idiot!' Davina's voice was sharp with irritation. 'Madeleine isn't the only woman in the world.'

For long, tense moments their eyes locked and Davina quivered inside, afraid of the fury she could feel radiating from his tense body. She flinched as he put out his hands to grasp her shoulders.

'It's the truth, of course,' he said softly. 'There *are* plenty of other women. My profession, in particular, is awash with them. But for a long time Madeleine has been my world—all I wanted.'

The gleam in his eyes hypnotised Davina. Their darkness held no laughter. They were full of something else that disturbed her badly, starting up the thumping in her chest again. She wasn't afraid, she assured herself, yet trickles of something very like fear ran along her nerves and down her spine, and suddenly she wished she had taken the trouble to dress properly, that she was wearing something more than a brief nightgown and the borrowed silk robe, even if it did cover her from throat to toes.

'Have you any idea, Davy, of what I mean by "wanting"?' went on Leo conversationally, as though his touch wasn't burning through the silk to her skin.

'I assume,' she said steadily, 'that you mean it in a sexual connotation.'

Leo laughed shortly, the sharp angles of his face very pronounced as his hands tightened on her shoulders. 'How clinical. But dead right.' He cocked his head on one side, his eyes running over her. 'You look different tonight, Davy.'

'I'm not in my school uniform.'

'I'd noticed.'

'And,' she added nastily, 'perhaps tonight you're actually rational enough to see me as an ordinary girl, instead of a—a means of ferreting out information.'

He took his hands away and sat back, eyeing her challengingly. 'You couldn't, by any chance, be a little bit jealous of Madeleine, Davy?'

Davina stared at him, aghast, then jumped up, awkward in her embarrassment. 'Casey wants to go out—I'd better let him into the garden for a moment.'

Leo sprang up to forestall her. 'I'll do it. You'll catch cold dressed like that.' He clicked his fingers to Casey and went out, leaving Davina to sit down on the hearthrug, her mind in turmoil. Her parents would be another hour or so yet. She should send Leo away. Yet this might be all she would ever have of him. After tonight she would probably never see him again. One hour alone with him wasn't all that much to ask, surely! She deserved it after the misery of the past week. Now that Leo was back to someone more like the man of the birthday dinner, it would do no harm to sit and chat with him. Even if Madeleine *was* the sole topic of conversation. Davina picked up the hairbrush and began to run it through the heavy strands of hair, looking up uncertainly as Leo came back.

'Casey opted for his bed in the kitchen,' he said, his eyes actually laughing again, she saw with relief. 'So I left him to it.' He held his hand out for the brush. 'Here. Give it to me.' He sat down on the sofa and turned her so that she leaned against his knees as he drew the brush gently through her hair.

Davina sat tense at first, hands clenched as Leo wielded the brush, but gradually she relaxed as Leo combed his fingers through her hair.

'Such a mane, Davy, and so many different colours. You're the first girl I've seen with striped hair,' he said teasingly.

'Needs cutting,' she said gruffly.

'No! Don't cut it. It's beautiful. There.' He smoothed a hand over it and a tremor ran along her nerves. 'It's dry now. Up you come.' And he leaned over to pull her up beside him.

Davina kept her eyes on her hands, unable to look at Leo, who was changed somehow. This was someone different from the man of her party, and the animated, friendly companion of her day with him at Hadfield Chase. Nor was he the tormented, jilted lover. She stole a look at him to find him studying her intently.

'When will your parents be home, Davy?' he asked.

'In an hour or so,' she said rashly, then halted. Fool! She should have said they were expected any minute. 'If you don't want to wait,' she rushed on, 'I'll tell them you called to say goodbye.'

Leo chuckled and took one of her hands in his. 'I'm in no hurry, Davy. And it seems a shame to go back to my solitary room in the Crown when you're all on your own here. Do you *want* me to go?' His eyes held hers and she shook her head dumbly. 'Then I'll stay a while,' he said, and slid his arm round her waist.

She should have told him she *did* want him to go, to take his arm away, that it wasn't fair to look at her like this.

'Madeleine——' she began, but Leo put a finger on her lips.

'To hell with Madeleine,' he said, unbelievably, and pulled her closer, frowning as he held her tight, seeing her clearly, she could tell, for the first time. 'You've lost weight, poppet—I feel ribs.' He brushed a fingertip along her cheekbone. 'And the shadows under these spectacular eyes—are they because of Sean and me?'

No, just you, she thought, but said nothing, letting him draw his own conclusions. He closed his eyes suddenly and tightened his arms about her.

'I've been a brute to you, little one, and I'm sorry, sorry. I must have been out of my mind to keep hounding you like that, day after day.'

Davina tried for lightness. 'It's an ill wind, Leo. My stock's gone up no end with the girls in school. They thought it was me you were after.' She smiled up at him shakily. 'Hilarious, isn't it?'

Leo's eyes opened. 'No,' he said fiercely. 'Not hilarious in the least.' And he bent his head to kiss her, just the way he did in all her fantasies. Only it wasn't the same at all. In her dreams his lips were gentle, reverent even, and his main emotion was gratitude. But now the scene was real his lips were seeking, searching, his tongue—oh, mercy, his tongue was in her mouth and his arms were suddenly iron bands that held her prisoner, until one of them loosened and his free hand slid between the lapels of the dressing-gown and pulled down the thin cotton of her nightgown. When his long, thin fingers found the curve of her breast, closed gently on a soft pink nipple, she threshed wildly, frightened now.

Dimly Davina could sense he wasn't making love only to her. All the pent-up emotion of Leo's past week was channelled now in her direction, as she had wanted, but she trembled wildly beneath his onslaught, certain he was pretending she was Madeleine. Then at some stage she stopped thinking altogether, no longer caring why he was making love to her. She was in his arms, for whatever reason, and the fright was gone, replaced by a warm, melting excitement. Her mouth opened, her body yielded and he gasped blindly and plundered her untried sweetness, assuaging all his hurt and pain in the trusting, unlooked-for response of her young body.

Then all too soon it was over. Leo tore himself away, lifted Davina by the elbows and thrust her into a corner of the sofa, breathing raggedly as he wrapped the worn red silk about her in silence. Gradually her breathing slowed and shame replaced passion, as she turned her head away. What in God's name had come over her? If

Leo hadn't called a halt she would have let him—let him . . . Disgust welled up inside her and she swallowed hard.

'Davy, I'm sorry,' Leo said at last.

'Not at all,' she managed. 'Perhaps you'll feel better now.'

His eyes narrowed. 'What do you mean?'

She shrugged carelessly. 'I imagine you felt in need of some kind of reparation from the Lennoxes—and I was the nearest.' Her composure, she felt, was quite remarkable, considering the tumult going on inside her. Disbelief glittered in the slitted dark eyes staring at her. 'You mean you actually thought I was exacting some form of payment for Sean's behaviour?'

It sounded far-fetched put like that, but Davina badly needed some kind of justification for her shaming lack of self-control. 'I thought you were entitled to a little substitute comfort,' she said, with lofty kindness.

'Did you now?' The words came through Leo's clenched teeth like grapeshot, and he jumped to his feet. 'I shan't stay to talk to your father, young lady. At this precise moment in time I've had it up to here with you Lennoxes.' He dragged on his leather jacket, glaring at her. 'Let me give you a word of advice, Davina. Don't go round offering "comfort" of that particular type to all and sundry or you're likely to get yourself in deep trouble. Not every man is blessed with my self-control.'

Davina felt sick at the distaste in his eyes. 'I think it's time you went.'

'So do I.' Leo wrenched the door open and gave her a smile that froze her to her bones. 'You can relax from now on, little girl. I won't trouble you again.' And he strode out into the hall and let himself out of the house and out of her life.

CHAPTER TWO

DESPITE his parting words, Leo Seymour had managed to trouble Davina a lot more than she would have liked over the years, nevertheless, and without any conscious effort on his part to do so, either. Davina scowled at the memory of many a sleepless night as she secured the glass windows separating the reception area from the waiting-room, annoyed that she hadn't been able to get Leo out of her mind all day. It was late, but the evening sun still shone brightly outside, where the rest of the world was doing normal summer things like walking and gardening and sitting outside pubs drinking long, cool drinks. She ran the tip of her tongue round her lips at the thought as she left the central citadel of the reception area, and dragged down the steel portcullis which protected the glass partitions at night. After tidying up the waiting-room she went along to the room of the one doctor still in the building. Dr Harvey, who looked as weary as she felt, glanced up from the medical records he was studying, surprised.

'Good God—you still here, Davina? Shouldn't you have knocked off a couple of hours ago?'

'When I finished in the office I took over in reception. Helen's little boy had a dental appointment.'

'Dammit, Davina, you're supposed to be the practice secretary, not general dogsbody!' Dr Harvey shook his head disapprovingly. 'Anyway I'll pack it in and get home so you can lock up.'

'Thank you, Doctor. Shall I put the answering machine through to your home now?'

'Fine,' he said absently, packing his bag. 'Rosemary's there, cooking something substantial, I devoutly hope.

I'm starving.'

So was Davina. She mentally reviewed the contents of her refrigerator as she returned to reception, not very optimistic about her own meal. All the shops would be shut by this time. She sighed, then poked out her tongue at the telephone as it rang before she could plug in the message giving Dr Harvey's number for emergencies. Davina picked up the receiver and said, 'Good evening, Hadfield Surgery.'

A frantic male voice cut in, babbling in sheer panic. 'For God's sake can you get a doctor here right now? This is the manager of the Manor Farm Hotel at Long Rise—the bloody chef's gone berserk.'

'Hold on, please,' she said, unperturbed. 'I'll put you through to Dr Harvey.'

'All right, Davina.' Dr Harvey took the receiver and spoke with calm authority to the distressed man at the other end, then put the phone down, resigned. 'Get through to Rosemary, will you? Tell her to put dinner back, then you can switch the phone through to her. This chef chappie has gone completely off his rocker by the sound of it—cornered a bunch of guests in the bar with a meat cleaver. Means I'll have to take him off to the psychiatric wing at Hadfield Hospital myself to commit him.'

'Oh, bad luck,' sympathised Davina. 'Not the ideal end to a hectic day like today.'

Most days were hectic at the practice, and she was glad when she finally locked up the building and set off on the walk home, pleased to be out in the fresh air to enjoy the remainder of the summer evening. She had more attention to spare for the peaceful scene now as she passed three inns of varying size and attraction, the village green, the pond with its mandatory ducks sailing on it in the sunset light, the small church with its square Norman tower. Earlier she had been too taken up with old memories to notice any of it, but at this time of day it was like a picture postcard, far removed from the violence of the scene at the hotel. Davina turned in at the gate of Ivy Cottage half-way down Glebe Lane. Only the ground floor was hers. The upper floor was a separate establishment with its own entrance, unoccupied for the moment because her landlord was doing it up with an eye to charging more rent. But for the time being, at least, the sizeable back garden was hers to enjoy alone. She unlocked her front door and submitted to a rapturous greeting from a very bleary-eyed Casey, who had plainly been fast asleep on the sofa, but now wanted a run in the garden. She flopped down on the rustic bench at the far end while the old dog ambled round the apple trees and investigated the syringa, which was starred with white blossom and gave out a heavenly scent in the warm summer evening. Davina breathed in appreciatively, then got up.

'Come on, Casey. Time for your dinner.' The old dog loped after her eagerly, and when he had been fed and was sound asleep again, Davina ran herself a bath and lay in it, relaxing at last, determined not to think of Leo Seymour any more. Next day was Saturday, but even so not a day to call her own. There were a couple of hours to put in at the practice, since it was her turn on the Saturday rota, after which she had rashly promised to take charge of the white-elephant stall at the church fête in the afternoon. As she ate scrambled eggs from a tray in front of the television, Davina felt distinctly regretful about the fête. A lazy afternoon to herself wouldn't have gone amiss.

Saturday morning surgery went off without a hitch next day, for once, with only two doctors presiding and Davina, plus Helen Bates, thirty-year-old mother of two, in attendance. Helen was agog to hear about the incident at the Manor Farm Hotel, incensed that she had gone home and missed all the excitement.

'There wasn't much *here,*' Davina assured her. 'Dr

Harvey said two men were injured, one with an injured arm, the other with concussion, but both were sent off to Hadfield Casualty for treatment. Apparently they were the two who tried a hand at subduing the manic chef.'

'What a carry-on!' Helen eyed her across the table. 'Still feel up to the fête this afternoon?'

'Of course. The Rector's wife, you might care to know, has given me strict instructions about wearing a dress which displays not only a hint of cleavage, but shows off my legs—something to catch the eye so the men will flock to buy the rubbish I'm required to sell.'

'Dear me—naughty Mrs Maybury! She never said anything like that to me.'

'Since you're on the home-made-cake stall it wouldn't matter if you wore a boiler-suit and a gorilla mask; everything sells in an hour or so anyway. By the way, is Lady Harbury opening the fête as usual?'

Helen shook her head as they went the rounds together, locking up. It seemed there was to be a celebrity, some actor or other who was doing the deed instead, since Lady Harbury had resigned the job due to increasing age.

'And sheer boredom, probably, hers and ours,' added the irrepressible Helen.

'What actor? Someone well known?' Davina brightened.

'No idea. It's all very last minute, because Lady Harbury's advancing years mysteriously overtook her only this week and poor Mrs Maybury had to do a lot of frenzied arm-twisting to persuade someone to take her place.'

Intrigued, Davina called in at the village shop on the way home for some groceries and whatever information Mrs Baker, the owner, and infallible source of local news, had to impart. It was discouraging. Apparently not even the actor could open the fête now, due to some accident. Disappointed, Davina went home to lunch sensibly off cheese and salad, then put on the only dress she possessed which remotely fitted Mrs Maybury's requirements.

'What do you think, Casey?' she asked when she was ready, and the dog panted gently, his tongue hanging out. 'I hope that's approval—it's so seldom I get a male panting after me that it's hard to tell.'

Nevertheless Davina was fairly satisfied with the cotton jersey dress, which had a narrow knee-length skirt, and a sleeveless bloused top with a lowish neckline. It showed a satisfactory amount of smooth tanned skin, and was in an eye-catching shade of sunshine-yellow, though from choice Davina would have opted for denims and T-shirt for selling dusty bric-a-brac. Ignoring Mrs Maybury's injunction to let her hair hang loose, she swept it all up to the crown of her head then braided it in one thick pigtail which swung between her shoulder blades, smiling as she remembered grumbling over having to wear it that way in school.

When she arrived at the Rectory the big rambling garden was already full of stalls, with sideshows in the paddock beyond. Helpers were milling everywhere, and Davina pitched in with a will, taking all kinds of objects from the cartons stacked behind her stall, which the Rector's wife had chosen because of its prime position between the cake-stall and the refreshment tent.

'So everyone has to pass you, my dear,' she said, highly delighted with Davina's appearance. 'You look splendid. Just the thing to attract the men in that dress—like a ray of sunshine!'

Davina wrapped herself in an apron and began dusting off her motley collection of wares, aided by the Rector's son Brian, who was recovering from the trauma of A-levels and grateful for a sympathetic ear for his woes. Helen waved from behind her array of goodies, winking as her husband Peter trudged off to man the coconut shy, his face filled with comic gloom, and at two o'clock sharp the outside world was let in, at which point the Rector bawled for quiet through his loudhailer so that he could introduce the celebrity who had kindly consented not only to open the fête, but to make a generous donation to the cause, which was money for repairs to the church tower. Davina took off her apron and rubber gloves and stood on tiptoe, trying to see over heads towards the makeshift dais where the mysterious 'celebrity' would make his speech. The Rector spoke experimentally into the microphone set up by the local electrician, then assumed his normal pulpit delivery to inform the assembled crowd that originally Mr John Wynne Jones, the famous actor, had agreed to open the fête, since he was engaged in filming at a location in the neighbourhood. Due to a very unfortunate accident only the day before . . . Suddenly the microphone went dead and Mr Maybury was left mouthing inaudibly; there were cheers from the crowd and the electrician darted forward to remedy the fault.

'Just who *is* this celebrity, Brian?' asked Davina.

'Some film director—makes arty sort of films——' The rest of Brian's remarks went unheard as Davina stared with mounting doom at the figure ascending the dais. His arm was in a sling, his hair was darker, and he was less thin than when she had last seen him; nevertheless the 'celebrity' was unmistakably Leo Seymour, just about the last man on earth Davina had any desire to meet again, now or any time. She retreated behind her stall, trying to keep out of range of Leo's dark eyes, which held very little laughter now, as far as she could see, even from a distance. He looked different: formidably elegant in what looked like a Gianni Versace suit, with a white shirt open at the neck and his tawny lion's mane very sleek and expertly cut.

She watched unhappily as Leo Seymour smiled down into the expectant faces of the crowd and made a

graceful apology for his role as substitute for John
Wynne Jones, who at this moment was in hospital. And
since, went on Leo, his recovery was vital to the
schedule of the film they were making together he had
insisted his leading actor take it easy for a day or two so
that shooting could resume as soon as possible. It was,
of course, Leo said smoothly, a great personal pleasure
to be able to act as stand-in and declare the St John's
church fête well and truly open.

Davina relaxed as the applause died away. Business
became brisk at all the stalls, including hers, to her
surprise, as people bargained for chipped china vases
and dog-eared paperbacks, and she was kept busy
wrapping up objects she was astounded anyone had the
least desire to buy. As she laughed and chatted to her
customers the shock of seeing Leo again slowly receded,
and she had time to wonder how he'd come by his
injury, and to feel grateful for it, since it was unlikely he
would linger at the fête in his condition. Probably Mrs
Maybury would ply him with tea and fancy cakes in the
peace and seclusion of the Rectory and his duty would
be done. But then Davina's heart sank as she saw that,
far from leaving early, Leo was actually moving from
stall to stall, accompanied by the Rector, who was
plainly bent on introducing him to every stallholder in
turn.

'Brian—can you . . .' Davina fumed in exasperation.
She had been about to ask the boy to hold the fort until
Leo was out of the way, but Brian was fast disappearing
towards the paddock with a group of his cronies to try
the delights of the sideshows. Mentally shoring up her
defences, Davina returned to the fray, extolling the
virtues of a singularly hideous china dog of unknown
breed.

'Oh, definitely Royal Worcester, Mrs Brackett,' she
said without batting an eyelid, 'but so old the mark has
worn from the base.'

The woman beat Davina down to half the asking price and bore her trophy off in triumph, and in the slight lull which followed Davina could see Leo at the next stall with the Rector, and stood frustrated, yearning for sudden invisibility.

'Ah, Davina, my dear,' said Mr Maybury. 'How very charming you look. Let me introduce Mr Seymour, who so kindly stepped into the breach for us today. Mr Seymour, allow me to present Miss Lennox.'

Leo stood motionless, staring at Davina, his face empty of expression, and there was a nasty little silence before Davina collected herself sufficiently to say 'How do you do,' in as colourless a voice as she could manage. He responded with a formal little bow in acknowledgement.

'No need for introductions in fact, Rector,' he said smoothly. 'I already know Davy. It's several years since we last met, I admit, but I think you could describe us as old friends.'

The Rector beamed. 'Splendid! No doubt you'll want to catch up on your news when Davina has sold all her treasures. But, in the meantime Mr Seymour, let's go in search of some refreshment.'

Leo gave Davina a smile she didn't care for at all, and strolled off, leaving her to deal with a group of clamouring children who were quarrelling over a pile of ancient comics. Brian came back eventually to ask if she wanted a tea-break, but she shook her head, asking him to fetch her a cold drink while she carried on. In some irrational way she felt safer behind her stall than outside it, where there was the possibility of bumping into Leo accidentally. With any luck he woud have gone by the time she was free to go home.

It was after five, but with almost everything sold, to her amazement, when Davina was able to make her escape. Helen had been full of excitement over the unexpected guest at the fête, pronouncing him a great improvement on old Lady Harbury, and utterly dumbfounded when Davina reluctantly confessed that she knew him. It was only by promising to give more details the following Monday that Davina was able to get away and go home to the sanctuary of Ivy Cottage, congratulating herself on a lucky escape. Her relief was premature. When she let Casey out into the garden she found Leo Seymour lounging on the rustic seat in the garden. The dog leapt towards him, barking, then stopped and began to fawn over the intruder in a way that did nothing to improve Davina's frame of mind. She stalked down the garden, calling Casey to heel, and Leo rose to his feet, smiling in a way that set her teeth on edge.

'Hello again, Davy,' he said. 'As the Rector said, I thought we should catch up on all our news.'

'I didn't expect to see you here,' she said curtly. 'How did you find out where I lived?'

'In a village like this? Come, come, Davy. Not exactly difficult. Mrs Maybury let it drop during our tea-party. Aren't you going to ask me in?' He gave a significant glance towards the cottages on either side. 'Or perhaps you'd prefer to talk out here? I really don't mind.'

Davina led the way into the house, defeated, and waved him to a chair in the small parlour. 'Would you care for some tea?' she asked stiffly.

'God, no! I'm awash with the stuff already.' He eyed her hopefully. 'I don't suppose you have anything more interesting?'

Without a word Davina went back into the kitchen and took two cans from the fridge. She poured lager into a tall glass, lemonade into another, then took them into the other room. 'All I've got, I'm afraid.'

'Perfect,' he said, tasting the lager, then eyed her lemonade. 'Have I taken the last one?'

'No. I don't drink lager myself.'

'You keep it for someone—a lover, perhaps?' Leo's

eyes were speculative. 'Does he live with you?'

'I live alone, and I don't have a lover. I do have one or two men-friends, if it's of any interest, and I generally keep a few cans of lager or beer for them.' Davina drank some lemonade, uncomfortable under Leo's unwavering scrutiny. She was fairly sure he wasn't feeling all that terrific, from the dark smudges under his eyes, and she noted a wince as Casey nudged his arm, begging to be stroked. She clicked her fingers at the dog, and reluctantly Casey plodded over to lie at her feet. 'Bad break?' she asked, as the silence began to lengthen.

'It isn't broken—just cut. I was told it would feel easier in a sling, but frankly the damn thing's beginning to throb like hell.' Leo drank thirstily, downing the rest of the lager.

'How did it happen?'

His eyes were sardonic. 'Davy, if I told you you'd never believe me in a million years.'

She smiled faintly. 'Did you, by any strange chance, barge into a bar yesterday where a maniacal chef was threatening the patrons with a meat-axe?'

He whistled in astonishment. 'How the hell did you get wind of that? The hotel manager practically went on bended knees for silence on the subject to protect the Manor Farm's reputation, not to mention its trade. Pity, really. The publicity would have done Jack—and the film—a power of good.'

'Jack?'

'John Wynne Jones, classical actor and one-time rugby player. He crash-tackled the chef, then I sat on the poor blighter's chest and got a gash in my arm for my pains—and I *do* mean pains!'

'How is Mr Wynne Jones?'

'His head met the base of the bar with an almighty crack, but apart from a black eye and a crashing headache he's not too bad. He could have fractured his skull, the idiot, but the X-ray was clear, thank God—a great relief, I can tell you!'

'You're very fond of him?'

Leo chuckled. 'Still naïve, Davy? Yes, I *do* like Jack; always have. But more important than that, I'm bloody relieved he's able to carry on filming so we don't waste the backers' money.'

'Ah!' Davina nodded, enlightened. 'I see.'

'I can't say I do. How the devil did you hear about it?'

'I work in the medical centre here in the village.'

Leo frowned. 'Are you the nurse there?'

Davina looked away. 'No. I'm the secretary. And I fill in on reception when necessary—even do some dispensing now and then.'

'But weren't you dead set on becoming a nurse at one time, Davy?'

'I was. I got as far as SEN right on target.'

'What happened?'

'I had a fall from a horse. Hurt my back, so no more nursing. I'm fully recovered,' she added hastily, 'but officially considered unsuitable for the rigours of hospital duties. So I took a course in shorthand and typing and so on, and now I'm a medical secretary.'

Leo's face softened. 'I'm sorry, Davy. Very sorry. I remember how much a hospital career meant to you.'

'It isn't the end of the world—and I'm still involved with things medical.' Davina met his eyes with meaning. 'I firmly believe we should get on with our lives as best we can, without allowing certain—setbacks to embitter and change one out of all recognition.'

The lids dropped over Leo's eyes and his mouth tightened, a very cynical smile playing at the corners. 'By which, Miss Lennox, I'm to infer that you think I lacked charity, even backbone, about a certain episode in my life. You think I should have been more philosophical and forgiving about the fact that your beloved brother Sean ran off with my intended bride!'

CHAPTER THREE

'IT TAKES two,' pointed out Davina, and collected his glass. 'Have another lager.' She went off to the kitchen quickly, glad of the excuse to get away from her visitor for a moment. Inside she was quaking like a half-set jelly and lingered over her task in an effort to pull herself together. It was utterly stupid to feel so guilty. The guilt was in no way hers. It was Sean's—and Madeleine's. Not that guilt was her only emotion. Seeing Leo again after all these years was nerve-racking, particularly on top of brooding over him so much the day before. She felt uncomfortable in his company, haunted by the memory of those heart-stopping moments in his arms all those years ago. Leo's attitude wasn't exactly reassuring, either. Older and more cynical he might be, but one thing seemed glaringly unchanged. He obviously still carried a blazing torch for Madeleine. Davina sighed. Some women were *femmes fatales* without even trying, and Madeleine Lennox, *née* Deane, was one of them.

When she returned to Leo his eyes looked very heavy as he took the glass from her. 'Thank you, Davy. Sorry I bit your head off. But coming across you so unexpectedly after all this time straight after last night's trauma was rather a shock.' He eyed her over his glass. 'And how is your famous journalist brother? No need to report on Madeleine, of course. Her starry progress is easy to follow.'

'Sean is fine as far as I know. He's just survived an earthquake and lived to tell the tale; quite literally, of course.' Davina sat down, her composure somewhat restored.

'He always was a lucky swine.' Leo stared broodingly into his glass. 'How are your parents, Davina?'

'Mother's well, but my father died last year,' she answered quietly. 'Mother sold the house. She lives in a flat near Sarah and Joe now, in Surrey, quite near Sean's place. She comes in very useful as baby-minder.'

Leo looked up swiftly. 'Sean and Madeleine have a child?'

'No, not yet. But Joe and Ben make up the deficit. So Mother more or less divides herself between Surrey and Manchester when needed, but still keeps her own little bolthole. To avoid over-exposure, as she puts it.'

Leo got up and crossed over to sit by Davina on the sofa, taking her hands in his. 'I'm very sorry about your father, Davy. I liked your parents very much.' His mouth twisted. 'I liked all your family, in fact, until——'

'Let's not talk about it,' said Davina flatly, feeling jumpy again. She wished Leo would go, let her get herself together again. She had honestly believed she was completely over him. God knew she had had long enough to try. But reading about him yesterday, and then seeing him so unexpectedly at the fête, had knocked her off balance. Now he was here in the same room it was frightening to find how well she remembered every last little thing about him, including her youthful idolatry. A fair number of men had figured in the adult Davina Lennox's life, but none had come even near to affecting her as deeply as Leo Seymour. Her ringside seat at the drama of jealousy and passion played out under her nose that long-ago autumn had armoured her very effectively against any serious attachments ever since. She pulled herself together, realising he was watching her face closely. 'Well then, Leo, what exactly brings you to this part of the world again?' She smiled at him brightly.

Leo's eyes laughed at her suddenly, in the old well-remembered way, dancing in his straight face. 'I am making a film, Miss Lennox, what else? It's the way I earn my crust, if you remember.'

'With a fair amount of butter and jam on top, as I hear it. I read bits about you in the Press.' She stopped, cursing herself, and he smiled sardonically.

'Ah yes; the Press. If it hadn't been for that first memorable intrusion into my life by a certain member of their happy band things would have been enormously different, wouldn't they? I would have been a much-married man by now, for one.'

'And you might still be the assistant to the assistant producer, or whatever, instead of one of our more successful film directors,' retorted Davina.

'Very true. None of us can avoid our own particular karma, I suppose. No doubt I sinned in some former incarnation. *Ergo* I was deprived of the lady of my choice in this life and then granted success in my career to redress the balance.' His eyes dropped to the expanse of smooth tanned thigh revealed by Davina's skirt. 'You know, you have very pretty legs, Davy. No—don't jump away like that. I'm not in the least likely to fall on you in ravening lust. I'm a quick study—I learned my lesson the first time.'

Which was letting her know he remembered everything too. Davina looked at him levelly. 'I'm glad to hear it. Though I wasn't really worried. I'm not your type. Your taste leans, or did once, to tall brunettes like Madeleine.'

Leo's face was expressionless. 'I feel I should also point out that I've got several stitches in my arm and bruises in places I won't even mention, all of which tend to have a rather subduing effect on any libidinous tendencies I might nurture for *any* lady, however ravishing. And in all sincerity, you've grown up into a very beautiful woman, Davy. A sight for sore eyes, believe me. A pity mine come as part of the same package as this blasted arm at the moment!'

Davina became suddenly brisk. 'Take your jacket off and let me have a look at it.'

He stared at her in alarm. 'Why? What are you going to do?'

'Check the dressing. Don't worry, coward, I'm not qualified to amputate. I'm only a nurse.'

Reluctantly Leo suffered himself to be helped out of his expensive jacket and shirt, then Davina led him into the kitchen and sat him on one of the stools at her minuscule little breakfast-bar while she removed the dressing on his arm and examined the wound.

'Close your eyes if you can't bear to look,' she ordered. 'H'm, very nice. Perfectly healthy. But I'll put on a fresh dressing, after which I'd advise you to keep your arm in the sling.' She went off to fetch her first-aid box, and ten minutes later Leo was settled on the sofa in the parlour again, fully dressed, looking pale but more relaxed.

'A ministering angel thou,' he murmured.

Davina handed him a cup of coffee laced with the brandy she kept for emergency, ignoring his remark. 'I don't know that you ought to be drinking spirits, really—but I don't suppose a small drop of cognac will do much harm.'

'Darling, it's doing a power of good,' he assured her, sipping with relish. 'You have very soothing, gentle hands, if I'm allowed to say so.'

'Yes. But cut out the "darling" bit, please.'

'Why?'

'It sounds so facile; as though you can't remember my name. Which, incidentally, is Davina. Nobody calls me Davy any more.'

'That's a pity. I like it. It brings back all sorts of pleasing pictures to my mind . . .' He smiled as she flinched. 'I meant, *Davy,* that I recall big, bright eyes and pink cheeks and a shaggy mop of striped hair.' He eyed the braid swinging past Davina's ear as she bent to take his cup. 'The stripes are still there, I see, but why do you scrape such beautiful hair back like that?'

Davina glanced pointedly at her watch. 'Isn't someone expecting you somewhere?' She broke off as the telephone rang, and excused herself to answer it. Greg Barrett's voice sounded in her ear, urgent and apologetic. He was the latest trainee at the practice, and her escort for the evening, but to his regret he had been roped in as duty doctor because Dr Harvey had gone down suddenly with a stomach bug.

'I could put your number on the answering machine and come over on the off chance nothing much will come up tonight,' Greg offered eagerly.

'I'm pretty tired anyway, Greg, after my stint at the fête. Let's leave it to another evening, and I'll settle for an early night.'

Since the telephone was in the kitchen, which was only a few feet away, there was no possibility of not being overheard, and when Davina rejoined Leo he grinned.

'Been stood up?'

She nodded, unperturbed. 'Comes of mixing with doctors. Social life in the medical profession tends to be uncertain.'

'Have dinner with me instead,' he said promptly.

'Break bread with the enemy, Leo?' Her smile was

mocking. 'I would have thought eating with a Lennox would choke you, even now.'

'I can't say a place at Sean's table would hold much attraction, but I've no quarrel with you, Davina. You did what you did because Sean forced you, as I know only too well. Not cricket, really, bullying his little sister into perjury.' Leo's eyes were hard.

'You've got the wrong end of the stick, Leo. It was Madeleine who made me do all the lying. Sean was all for confronting you and having it out with you— apologising, even.'

Leo laughed shortly. *'Apologising!* You mean he actually wanted to say how sorry he was for making off with my woman? Did he expect me to shake hands and be frightfully British and stiff-upper-lip about it all?'

'Leo,' said Davina quietly. 'Contrary to popular belief, it just isn't possible to run off with someone who doesn't want to be run off with—not without a gun, or the threat of grievous bodily harm, or something. Sean didn't need anything like that, believe me. Madeleine was so much in love with him she could hardly breathe. It was uncomfortable to be in their company, frankly. *My* sympathies were all with you.' She smiled bleakly. 'I really worshipped you, Leo. I fell flat on my face in the throes of puppy love the moment you walked through our front door.' She stopped, sorry she had said so much as Leo leaned forward, his eyes gleaming.

'Did you, Davy? I suspected you weren't exactly indifferent to me, of course.' He paused delicately. 'Am I allowed to ask why, if you *did* feel something towards me, you sent me packing when I, er, sought a little balm from you for my wounds?'

'Even to a stupid little teenager it wasn't flattering to be used as a substitute for someone else.' Davina's voice was bitter. 'What a mass of seething emotions we all were, to be sure. I yearned for you. You were frothing at the mouth over Madeleine, while she and Sean were panting after each other.'

Leo's face was stiff with distaste. 'You make it sound very sordid. You forget, I was very much in love with Madeleine.'

'Forget? Me?' She looked him in the eye. 'For heaven's sake let's stop raking up the past. Time's going on, and I just can't believe someone, somewhere, isn't expecting Mr Leo Seymour tonight.'

'Not a soul.' Leo leaned back on the couch, crossing his long legs. 'They've kept Jack in hospital until tomorrow and the rest of the unit won't be here until Monday, so here I am, injured, alone and unwanted. Are you going to kick me out?' He eyed her challengingly. 'Forgive me for mentioning it, but even with one of my arms out of action I don't think you're up to it if I refuse to go.'

Davina acknowledged the truth of this. Her bulges, like her adolescent illusions, had never returned after parting from Leo, and her neat, trim figure weighed the ideal amount necessary for her five-foot-nothing frame. 'You forget I was a nurse, Leo. I'm quite used to manhandling recalcitrant male patients. But I won't resort to strong-arm tactics,' she assured him. 'If you stay you'll have to put up with whatever I was going to have for supper. I'm certainly not about to eat out anywhere locally with you. And if you do stay you'll have to leave early. This is a small village, and I'm quite well known here because of where I work. I've no intention of earning an unwarranted reputation because the celebrity film director did me the honour of coming to see me.'

'But the Rector knows we're old friends,' he reminded her. 'Apart from which we're linked inextricably, you might say, by past experience.'

'One I'd give much to forget, believe me! It gives me no pleasure to remember the hideous fuss you made when Madeleine left you flat. If it's any comfort to you my parents were furious too—not only because they liked you, but because Sean sneaked home in their absence that fateful weekend to lie low with Madeleine. I hated every minute of it.'

'I know you did. Only the fact that you were so sick about what was happening made me give up and go away.' His eyes hardened. 'Don't distress yourself, Davy. It's many a long year since then. I wanted to kill them both—and myself—at the time, but the most dramatic thing to happen in actual fact was that I caught a cold. Then, as you know, the film was cancelled, and everything fell apart for me for a while. The house at Hadfield Chase has remained inviolate ever since—until now.'

Davina raised her eyebrows. 'Is that how you happen to be in the area? To film something else at Hadfield Chase?'

'Not something else. The same film; Byron, Augusta Leigh, John Wynne Jones and all. Only this time Miss Madeleine Deane is not part of the cast.' He gave her a mocking grin.

'Not possible, anyway. Madeleine's appearing in a play in the West End.' Davina got up, switching on the television to entertain him, and excused herself to prepare a meal.

The fête had yielded up a basketful of goodies in the way of salad vegetables and pickles and mayonnaise, and a very luscious-looking chocolate cake Helen had saved for her from the cake-stall. Davina quickly put together an appetising cold supper, and left everything ready on the little bar in the kitchen while she went back to Leo, who was sprawled, relaxed, on the sofa, watching a newscast.

'Give me a few minutes to shower, then I'll feed you,' she said. 'After my session on the white elephant stall I feel scruffy.'

'You don't look it,' he said promptly, his eyes laughing again. 'Certainly not more than I do, since Casey refuses to let me occupy the sofa alone. I detect a distinct aroma of dog about my person.'

Davina grinned. 'Sorry about that. He's rather possessive about that sofa. Be an angel and take him out in the garden while I wash, will you?'

'Won't the neighbours talk?' Leo heaved himself to his feet, wincing at the pain in his arm.

'Not if you're out there with Casey. It's in here with me that's more likely to cause tongues to wag. Shan't be long.'

She wasn't. Five minutes to shower, five minutes to slap a spot of eyeshadow and blusher on her face, brush her hair out loose as Leo had asked, then a scramble into canary-yellow cotton trousers and jade-green shirt and she was running downstairs again, just as Leo strolled in from the garden. His eyes gleamed as he looked her up and down.

'You look rather gorgeous, Miss Lennox, if I may say so!'

'Oh you may, you may. I love flattery. Do you want a wash before supper?'

Leo disengaged himself from Casey long enough to take his turn in the bathroom, and by the time he came back the old dog had been fed and banished to his bed, and Davina had the meal ready on a small table drawn up to the sofa.

'I've chopped up the salad so you can eat everything with a fork,' she said matter-of-factly, and Leo let himself down with care, smiling at her with mock respect.

'Are you always so terrifyingly efficient?'

'I'm hospital-trained, remember.'

'Do you miss all that, Davy?'

'Yes.' She handed him a plate of prawn salad and he took it absently, his eyes on her composed face.

'You've really grown up, Davy, haven't you?'

'I should hope so by this time.' She changed the subject. 'Now tell me all about this film, then.'

Leo took his cue obediently, and while they ate answered all her questions, adding that seven years had done little to John Wynne Jones's looks but had contributed considerably to his reputation as an actor, which augured well for the success of the film. The section at Hadfield Chase was due to be filmed almost at once, or at least as soon as the leading actor was fit enough after his tangle with the unfortunate chef at the hotel.

'Bloody marvellous,' sighed Leo in exasperation. 'Jack never gave it a minute's thought; he threw himself across the room as if he were scoring a try at Cardiff Arms Park, so I just had to pitch in and lend a hand.'

'You needn't have done it so literally!'

'Very true. Next time I'll just stand on the side-lines and cheer Jack on instead.' He held out his empty plate. 'I enjoyed that. Could I have some more, please?'

Davina was surprised to find she was rather enjoying herself. After years of never thinking of Leo Seymour any more than she could possibly help, seeing him at the fête earlier had nearly given her heart failure hard on the heels of the item in the newspaper. His appearance at the cottage later had been the final straw. She could think of no logical motive for his seeking her out, other than some kind of revenge, perhaps, for the simple reason that she was Sean's sister. Yet for the moment he seemed friendly enough, and perfectly happy consuming the simplest of suppers in her small parlour, which could hardly bear much resemblance to the type of place he normally frequented. The Manor Farm Hotel at Long Rise, for all its rural location, was in the luxury bracket, and Davina had never even aspired to a meal there on her salary, neither had any of her escorts.

'This is a nice little nest of yours, Davy,' observed Leo, almost as though he had read her mind. 'Who lives upstairs?'

'Nobody for the moment. My landlord has just finished doing it up so that he can get more rent for it. It's much more luxurious than this—enlarged and extended, and two of the rooms knocked into one, and the new bathroom's the talk of the village. Very nice, but I'm perfectly happy with my more humble bit—*and* its rent. Besides, I need a ground-floor flat for when Casey comes to stay with me.'

'He's not a fixture then?'

'No. He lives with Mother. But he's too old to go to kennels when she's off on her rounds to her babies, so he comes here to me. Have some cake while I make coffee.'

Davina could feel Leo's eyes on her as she took the used plates back to the kitchen and made cups of instant coffee for them both. She wished he would watch television, or play with Casey, but Casey was fast asleep, and Leo seemed to find her face much more interesting than anything on the television screen.

'This guy who stood you up tonight,' he said, as she sat down again. 'Is he a permanent arrangement?'

'Happy-ever-after prospect, you mean?' She shook her head. 'No. Pleasant company for an evening out, that's all.'

'Haven't you ever been in love, Davy? The real

McCoy, I mean; romance, passion, and all that sort of thing?'

'Oh yes, once. And I do mean once! As an experience it was useful, if only in convincing me it was too painful to risk repeating. I've steered clear of *grande passions* since. Much too wearing.'

'I can sympathise.' Leo looked at his watch. 'I should go.'

'What are you doing for transport?'

'My driver's down at the Huntsman in the village, drinking lemonade, I trust, waiting for my call to drive me back to the hotel at Long Rise. I'm not up to driving at the moment, with this arm. May I use the phone?'

Davina watched Leo's tall figure as he stood at the telephone, thinking how different he looked now. The intervening years had taken the eagerness from his face, etching a few cynical lines to make up the deficit, and he was heavier than he had been, his bones better covered. More money and better living, thought Davina.

'Frank will be here in a few minutes,' Leo said when he came back to her. 'Shall I see you again, Davy?'

She looked at him thoughtfully. 'I don't imagine so. You'll be busy with your film. Besides, I find it hard to believe you really want to fraternise with a Lennox.'

'True. "Fraternise" smacks of brotherly sentiments, and I'm short of those where Sean's concerned. But I've no quarrel with you, Davy.' Leo smiled. 'Can't we be friends?'

Davina was silent for a moment or two. 'No,' she said slowly at last. 'I don't honestly think we can. Our previous acquaintance can hardly count as much of a basis for friendship, one way and another.'

He frowned. 'Can't we put that episode behind us and just go on from here?'

'My last recollection of you, Leo Seymour, is a

violently angry young man who hounded me for days, then decided to turn his physical attentions towards me as the finishing touch.' Davina's clear, amber eyes met his without evasion. 'You made my life a misery. And for something which wasn't my fault, but Madeleine's.'

'And Sean's,' he pointed out curtly.

'And Sean's. But it takes two. I had nothing to do with any of it. You made me very unhappy, Leo. And what's more, you never even realised you were doing it, you were so wrapped up in your own misery.'

Leo sat down on the sofa beside her, his eyes sombre as they met hers. 'Until that last night I never gave a thought to what it was doing to you, Davy. If it's any consolation, I'm sorry, very sorry. I suppose I felt you were the only hope I had of finding out where Madeleine was. I could hardly ask your parents. Can you forgive me after all this time?'

She looked away. 'Of course. None of it matters now. Water under the bridge.'

'Then may I see you again?' he said at once.

'No,' she said flatly. 'I live in a very circumscribed community. In a village one has no secrets. If my name was linked with a glamorous man like you everyone would think the worst.'

'Glamorous!' He eyed her with distaste.

'Yes. If not you, your job.'

'So that's it then. I must shake hands, say thank you for having me and never darken your door again!' Leo jumped to his feet, his face set and angry.

'You don't *have* to shake hands if you don't want to.'

'No, I don't. I can think of something I'd much prefer.' He pulled her to her feet, kissing her hard before she had time to dodge.

Davina freed herself forcibly by the simple expedient of tugging at his injured arm, and Leo jumped away, cursing, his face pale as he glared at her.

'I thought nurses tried to heal people, not injure them beyond repair. You've probably pulled my bloody stitches out, woman!'

'Highly unlikely,' said Davina, unmoved, then sighed with exaggerated relief as the doorbell rang. 'Thank goodness, that must be your driver.'

'You needn't be so hell-fired eager to get rid of me,' said Leo bitterly. 'You Lennoxes do damn all for my self-esteem, one way and another.'

'Then you'd better steer clear of us. I didn't invite you here, Leo. You came of your own accord—no doubt intent on hearing the latest news of Madeleine. I'm not keen on being used as go-between, for whatever purpose. You can find out about her from your usual reliable sources, not me.' Her mouth tightened with distaste. 'Pig-in-the-middle isn't a role that appeals.'

Leo loomed over her, anger in his cold eyes. 'You're talking utter nonsense. Is it so impossible to believe that I came here solely to see *you*—with absolutely no ulterior motive?'

'Frankly, yes, I'm not seventeen and wet behind the ears any more, Leo.' She nodded towards the door as the bell rang again. 'You'd better be off—your driver's getting impatient.'

'He can wait.' Leo bent to pick up his jacket. 'So it's end of story then. A pity, since you liked me once.'

'That was a long time ago. Women change.'

'Isn't that the truth!' Leo turned to go, then hesitated. 'Odd, though. I would have bet my last penny *you'd* have been different, that we could still have been friends.'

'After seven years without my friendship, I don't imagine your life will be ruined without it from now on.' Davina went to the door to open it to the man standing patiently outside. 'Good evening,' she said to him courteously. 'Mr Seymour's ready to leave now.' She caught Casey by the collar as he woke up to the fact that someone was at the door, then held out her other hand in full view of the driver. 'Goodbye, Leo. Take care of that arm.'

'Goodbye, Davy.' Leo shook her hand formally. 'Thank you for tending my wounds, and giving me supper. It's been very interesting to meet you again. And to find out where you live.' He gave her an unsettling smile, then turned to the driver. 'Lead on then, Frank, and for God's sake drive carefully. One way and another I feel distinctly fragile.'

CHAPTER FOUR

DAVINA had a trying time once she was back at work. Helen probed unmercifully about her connection with Leo Seymour, and the general interest aroused in everyone on the subject drove Davina to drinking her coffee alone at her desk for a day or two, pleading pressure of work. Her only answer to all the questions was the unvarnished truth, as far as it went, that Leo Seymour had known her brother at college, and had looked her up after the fête to catch up on the family news. It would have been useless to try to keep his visit secret, since his driver had spent a couple of hours in the Huntsman, and after a day or two the teasing stopped and the incident was forgotten by the staff of the medical practice. For Davina it was much more difficult. Just seeing Leo again had brought back memories and feelings she had thought long forgotten.

'Long since, and it is better so. Oh, love, ere I remember, go'. Davina remembered the lines only too well. Byron, her least favourite poet, but in this instance very apt in all ways since Leo was making a film about the man, and because her initial reaction to the sight of Leo at the fête had knocked her for six. One incredulous look at him had affected her in very much the same way as on her seventeenth birthday. The feeling had been fleeting, and summarily quashed, but there was no point in deluding herself that dismay had been her sole emotion. Shock too, she told herself firmly, bringing back all the misery of unrequited puppy love, not to mention echoes of the uproar in the Lennox household over Sean and Madeleine. It had taken years of discipline to wipe out the memory of Leo Seymour. After that last evening, when he had made love to her so unforgettably, she had worked hard to convince herself she never wanted to lay eyes on him again. Her wish had been granted until now. She had read about Leo, gone to see his films out of curiosity, but never mentioned his name. Yet somehow, no matter how hard she tried, she could never quite dismiss Leo from the deepest inner recesses of her mind, making acceptance of Madeleine, even when finally married to Sean, very difficult. It had been a relief for Davina to get away from home when she eventually started work at the hospital in Birmingham, and it was years later, when a fall from a horse at the riding-stables kept Davina home for a long period while she convalesced, before she saw much of Madeleine, who came with Sean to visit the invalid.

Sometimes Davina felt her ultra-rapid recovery from her back injury had been owing to her urgent desire to escape from home and family, despite her love for her parents. Even when the final blow fell, and her nursing career was pronounced no longer possible, she promptly enrolled in a secretarial school, and the moment she was qualified had the great good fortune to get the job at the medical practice near Hadfield. It came as manna from heaven, too far away from home to travel daily, but near enough to see her parents often, and demanding enough for her work to serve as an excuse any time there was a family gathering she wanted to avoid. Yet when her father died a short while later, and her mother decided to sell The Laurels, Davina felt illogically bereft and deserted once there was no family home to go back to any more.

She shook herself out of her reverie, annoyed to find

herself dwelling on things best forgotten. Leo's intrusion into her well-ordered existence was a nuisance, nothing more. She said as much to her mother during the weekly telephone call, describing his visit in a flippant, jokey way that disguised her real feelings rather successfully, she thought.

'Upset you, did it?' demanded Margaret Lennox.

Davina sighed, exasperated. She might have known her mother's powers of perception would extend even down a telephone wire. 'He didn't *upset* me, Mother, but I admit I could have done without seeing him, just the same.'

'I trust he wasn't unpleasant!'

'Not in the least. He said he wanted to be friends, in fact.'

'Really? And what did you say to that?'

'No.'

Margaret Lennox sighed. 'You might try to be a little less inflexible, Davina.'

'I am, as a rule. But not in this particular instance. Don't worry. I'm not likely to see him again.'

The week was a busy one. Two of the staff were away on their annual holiday, and Davina put in extra time in reception to fill in for them once her office duties were done. She played tennis some evenings at the local club, went out with Greg Barrett, as promised, to make up for their broken date, and led what had become a fairly normal life since her advent in the village. At the weekend she joined Helen and Peter Bates and their children on a Saturday picnic, went out for dinner again with Greg in the evening, and luxuriated in an extra couple of hours in bed on Sunday morning, until Casey's demands to be let out could be ignored no longer. Yawning, Davina went barefoot to open the kitchen door into the garden, and the dog leapt out, barking suddenly. Davina pushed her hair out of her eyes and gasped. A man stood outside her door, hand raised, about to knock on it. He was tall, with wide, muscular shoulders and slim hips, and had longish, curly black hair and deep-set black eyes in a face which escaped sheer beauty only by virtue of a wide mouth and a large piece of sticking plaster on the forehead. He was barefoot like herself, dressed in a torn white sweatshirt and tattered tight denims, and he was smiling at her in undisguised delight.

'Hello,' he said. 'You must be Davy.'

She stared at him, recognition dawning in her eyes before she allowed them to travel deliberately down to his bare feet, then back up to the smiling face she had seen many times before on the cinema and television screen, but had never expected to see in her own back garden. 'You don't have a club foot, I note; nevertheless I believe I'm honoured by a visit from Lord Byron himself, am I not?' She smiled at him demurely. 'Should I shake your hand or ask for your autograph, Mr Wynne Jones?'

'Jack, please!' He took her hand in his, the grin on his face frankly admiring. 'How do you do, Miss Lennox, or may I call you Davy?'

'Davina, please!' she mimicked, then frowned. 'But what on earth are you doing *here?*'

'He's supposed to be borrowing some coffee,' yelled a voice from above, and Davina looked up, startled, to see Leo leaning out of the window on the upper floor of the cottage, forgetting her hand was still clasped in that of the man considered by many to be the second Richard Burton. Davina craned her neck to get a better look. 'What *are* you doing up there, Leo?' she demanded indignantly.

'Enjoying the view,' was the caustic reply and Davina

flushed, suddenly conscious that her sole garment was a striped cotton nightshirt. The Welsh actor laughed as Leo's head withdrew.

'He's just moved into the flat upstairs,' he informed Davina, whose jaw dropped at the news. 'Fantastic luck your telling him it was empty. It's a bit difficult finding any sort of accommodation in these parts.'

'You mean Leo Seymour's actually going to live *here?*'

He nodded. 'I helped him move in yesterday afternoon. I don't think you were around.'

'I wasn't.' Davina eyed him questioningly. 'Are you going to share with him?'

'My dear girl, what *are* you suggesting?' The handsome face fairly radiated laughter. 'Honest Injun, darling, Leo and I are just good friends, even if I did sleep on his sofa last night. We were done in after heaving furniture around all day, so we went down to the Bull for a pie and a pint, then came back here to crash out.'

Davina recalled hearing noise upstairs the evening before while she was getting ready to go out, but had assumed it was Sam Tanner, her landlord, putting the finishing touches to the renovated flat. And all the time it had been Leo taking up residence right over her head, in the very same house. 'Why did I open my big mouth?' she said bitterly, and Jack looked startled.

'You don't fancy Leo as a neighbour?'

She shrugged. 'Nothing to do with me who rents Sam Tanner's property. I just thought it was a bit downmarket for the trendy film director. I imagined you all in a five-star hotel discussing the day's shooting over a champagne supper.'

'You've been reading the Sunday glossies, darling. Anyway, we *were* in a hotel at first but the chef ran amok, then some of us got food poisoning, by which time Leo was getting restive, thinking the damn film was hexed this time as well. Honest to God, if it were the Scottish play it couldn't have worse luck.'

Davina chuckled. 'What a superstitious lot you actors are! Afraid to say the actual word *Macbeth*——'

'For pity's sake, *cariad,*' implored John Wynne Jones, rolling his magnificent eyes. 'Don't joke about it!'

Davina decided it was time to make herself more respectable. 'Anyway, come in and I'll get you the coffee.' She smiled suddenly. 'Or if you'll hang on a minute while I wash, I'll make you some.'

His face lit up and he followed her inside with alacrity. 'Better still. I'll put the kettle on.'

Davina flew to brush her teeth and hair and splash water on her face, while a very resonant voice sang Welsh hymns in her kitchen. She grinned, picturing Helen's face if she were to walk in at that moment, then pulled on her short towelling robe and went back barefoot to the kitchen to rejoin the exotic visitor. They were both perched on kitchen stools, laughing immoderately over a bawdy theatrical anecdote, when Leo stalked through the door, displeasure in every line of his face.

'You,' he said acidly to Jack, 'were supposed to borrow some coffee, not stay to breakfast.'

Jack spread his hands philosophically. 'Don't be a killjoy, Leo. Come and join us.'

'Yes,' echoed Davina sweetly. *'Do* join us, Leo. I'm longing to hear how you managed to keep Sam Tanner quiet about his new tenant.'

Leo shrugged carelessly. 'Bribery. Do you mind?'

'Yes. It's been rather nice here these past few weeks entirely on my own. Peaceful.'

'I shan't make much noise,' he assured her blandly. 'I own a separate entrance. My comings and goings will be conducted with absolute stealth, Davy, I swear.'

'How reassuring.' Davina turned away deliberately to smile at the actor. 'And what about you, Jack? Where are you going to put up?'

'Lady Harbury has a lodge vacant pro tem, and I am to be allowed to occupy it while we're filming.' Jack smiled mischievously. 'I gather she wasn't keen on letting it to an actor person at first—until she met me. She changed her mind when I used a little persuasion.'

'I'm sure she did.' Davina grinned, privately convinced that most women would grant John Wynne Jones anything he wanted if he troubled himself to persuade them. Or even if he didn't. Leo intercepted her look, evidently reading her mind with ease. His lips tightened in disapproval as his eyes dropped to her slim tanned legs, rather a lot of which were on display as she perched on her tall stool.

'It seemed pointless to wait for more plagues to try us,' he said shortly, 'so everyone's found new accommodation where they can. Hearing about this place from you just happened to be a lucky chance as far as I was concerned.'

'Very lucky,' observed Jack enviously. 'Only wish I'd heard of it first, old son. Anyway, God knows we don't want the damn film folding up again this time. If we wait another seven years I'll be a bit long in the tooth to play Byron. Not that anything *should* go wrong,' he added. 'The money's secure this time round, the location is fixed, and it's a different leading lady——' He halted, his expressive face vividly penitent. 'Oh, hell, Leo, sorry; my big mouth——'

'Don't worry,' Leo assured him blandly. 'You needn't mind Davy. It was her brother who ran off with

Madeleine, after all, so it's all in the family, as it were. No dark secrets between us, are there, sweetheart?' And to Davina's chagrin Leo slid an arm round her waist and dropped a kiss on her hair, and John Wynne Jones's black eyes gleamed. He gave them a knowing look and slid gracefully off the stool, drinking the remains of his coffee in one gulp.

'I'll let Davina make *you* some coffee now, friend,' he said, and prepared to depart.

Davina jumped down, annoyed by Leo's proprietary attitude. 'No need. Here's a spare jar,' she said briskly, reaching up into a cupboard. 'You may take it with my blessing. It's time I got dressed.'

'High time,' agreed Leo distantly, and took the coffee from her. 'I'll return this as soon as possible.'

'Oh, please don't bother,' she said brightly. 'Look on it as a moving-in present.'

Jack looked on with deep interest as Leo and Davina stared at each other. Finally Leo murmured conventional thanks, the actor expressed his appreciation of Davina's hospitality, then the two men left, leaving Davina feeling oddly restless for the entire day.

For the second Monday in succession life was hard for Davina at the practice. All the world seemed to know Leo Seymour had moved into the upper floor of Ivy Cottage, and Helen, in particular, was agog to hear the details. Davina said firmly there weren't any details. The two flats in the cottage were entirely separate, and it was quite probable she and Leo would see each other very little.

'Oh, come on!' protested Helen. 'A gorgeous man like that living in the same house and you can't manage to bump into him accidentally on purpose, Davina? Pull the other one!'

Davina headed her off with the news that John Wynne Jones was living in Lady Harbury's lodge while the film was being shot at Hadfield Chase, and the entire female staff of the medical centre was entranced, though Davina left out any mention of the breakfast episode the day before.

To her surprise it was some time before the inevitable encounter with Leo finally occurred. The entire week went by without even a glimpse of him, though sometimes late at night Davina heard him moving overhead as she tried to get to sleep. To her intense annoyance she found she was on edge all the time at home now Leo lived under the same roof, and rather mortified to find she was disappointed when the expected meeting never happened. To show how unmoved she was by Leo's strict observance of stealth and privacy, Davina went out three times with Greg Barrett in one week, which had variably satisfactory results. Her colleagues at the practice turned from curiosity about Leo to speculation about her relationship with the nice young trainee doctor, which was some sort of relief, but unfortunately Greg himself mistook her new enthusiasm for his company for something warmer. He proved difficult to send away late the following Sunday evening, after he brought her home from a pleasant evening at an inn on the banks of the River Avon. When they reached Ivy Cottage Greg assumed quite matter-of-factly that he would be allowed to stay.

Davina tried tact. 'It was a lovely evening, Greg. Thank you.' She yawned delicately, smiling at him. 'Gosh, I'm sleepy. Time to say goodnight, God bless, I think.'

Greg, a fair, stalwart young man with prominent blue eyes, looked startled. 'You mean you want me to go home *now?* Not even a cup of coffee?'

Davina was pretty certain coffee was by no means all Greg had in mind. 'Tomorrow's another day, Doctor. You and I both need our beauty sleep.'

Greg took her by the shoulders and looked down at her with a cajoling smile. 'Couldn't we get our beauty sleep together?'

Davina's heart sank. 'Not wise, Greg. Not in a village like this, when we both work at the practice.'

'Who's to know?' Greg looked at his watch. 'It's only a few minutes past eleven, Davina. If my first suggestion isn't on, couldn't I come in for just a hour, at least. I promise I'll do the Cinderella bit and rush off at midnight, if you must keep to the proprieties.'

Davina shook her head, nettled at his assumption that the proprieties were her only consideration. 'Sorry, Greg. Nothing doing.' And she turned away to open the door, but he was too quick for her. To her fury she suddenly found herself in the grasp of a very annoyed young man determined to end the evening in the way he had expected it to end all along. He picked her up with the obvious intention of barging through her front door and straight through to her bedroom. He reckoned without Casey, who forgot his advancing years and launched himself at the struggling couple, fastening his teeth round the young doctor's wrist, whereupon Davina was summarily dropped on the floor, while her would-be lover howled with pain and tried to beat off the snarling dog.

'Need any help, Davy?'

Davina looked up, mortified, to see Leo leaning in the doorway, surveying the scene with detached interest. Before she could say a word he bent and scooped her up, setting her gently on her feet before he turned his attention to the scarlet-faced young man still struggling to free himself from the dog. Leo clicked his fingers and said,

'Here boy, that's enough. Come here, Casey. Sit.' Casey relinquished his grip with one last warning growl and moved obediently to sit by Leo's bare foot, panting slightly and looking absurdly pleased with himself.

'Sorry about that, Greg,' Davina sighed as she noticed the young doctor's wrist was bleeding slightly. 'Are your tetanus shots up to date?'

'Yes.' Greg Barrett eyed Leo angrily. 'I apologise, Davina,' he added, and looked pointedly at Leo's casual garb, which consisted only of a pair of ancient white shorts. 'I'll bid you goodnight.'

Under the circumstances introductions seemed superfluous, but Davina felt obliged to make them nonetheless. The men gave each other unsmiling nods, and since Leo was very obviously determined to hold his ground, Greg took his leave with only the curtest of goodnights to the dishevelled girl, pointedly ignoring Leo, whose fingers were hooked through Casey's collar, since the dog was still showing signs of hostility towards the departing visitor.

Davina shut the door and leaned against it, feeling tired and embarrassed, and painfully aware of bruises in unseen places after her encounter with the floor. 'Thank you,' she said without enthusiasm. 'But your intervention was quite unnecessary. I could have coped.'

Leo released the dog, patting Casey's head affectionately. 'I'm sure you could—with good old Casey's help. But what happens when the dog goes back to your mother?'

'Nothing. The incident you walked in on tonight was

a one-off, I assure you. Fighting for my honour on my own doorstep is not a regular occurrence.' Davina sighed, and tried to smooth her hair, which had come undone from its upswept knot in the struggle. 'I don't wish to be ungrateful, Leo, but I would have managed that little scene much better without your help.'

'By which I assume you mean interference.' Leo shrugged gracefully. 'Sorry, Davy. But I was worried. You didn't look—or sound—like someone willing to be swept off her feet. I was reading by the open window upstairs and heard the whole thing. I honestly didn't intend to intrude, but it sounded as though you were about to be—er—ravished whether you liked it or not, so I thought I'd better see if you needed reinforcements. I'd reckoned without Casey.' He leaned down to fondle the dog. 'Good old boy. Not too old to protect your mistress, are you, old son?'

For once in her life Davina felt in sore need of a stiff drink, but since there was nothing alcoholic in the house she went towards the kitchen to fill up the kettle. 'Coffee, Leo?'

'You could do with something stronger, by the look of you. Come upstairs and have a brandy.'

She looked at him with suspicion. 'I'm not sure that's a good idea,' she muttered ungraciously.

His eyes lit with the smile she remembered so well. 'Bring Casey. He's already demonstrated his efficiency as chaperon.'

Davina was more shaken by Greg's unexpected behaviour than she was willing to admit, and suddenly the prospect of a drink and some company was very appealing. 'All right, Leo, I will. Thank you. But Casey doesn't have to come too. I hardly think you're likely to emulate young Dr Barrett.'

Leo grinned as Davina settled Casey in his bed. 'You're right. His bedside manner could use a little polish!'

CHAPTER FIVE

THE upper floor of Ivy Cottage bore very little resemblance to Davina's half. She whistled inelegantly as they reached the top of the stairs.

'Sam Tanner let you have it unfurnished, then.'

'I pay him the same price, but frankly I wasn't very struck by his bits and pieces, so I brought down one or two things from my place in town.' Leo waved her ahead of him into his domain, which appeared to be all one apartment, except for a door at the far end, which Davina presumed must be the bathroom.

Leo's taste was good, she conceded. A bed occupied one end of the room, the rest of which was sparsely furnished with sofa and chairs, a desk, a cupboard in dark, carved wood, and a heavy carved screen, both of which looked old and valuable. Even the carpet had an air of Persia, with subtle, faded colours nothing like the one Sam Tanner had put down originally.

'Nowhere to cook?' asked Davina.

'There's a sort of cupboard thing over there behind the screen, but it only hides a fridge, a kettle and a microwave oven. I'm nothing of a cook.' Leo opened the cupboard, revealing a portable television set, rows of books and a shelf of assorted bottles. 'Brandy, whisky, gin, vodka——'

'A very small brandy, please, with something to dilute it, if you have it.'

He looked at her searchingly. 'You're pale under that tan. Better take it neat, Davy. You still look a bit shaken.'

'I am,' she admitted. 'Shattered, to be honest. Who would have thought a caveman lurked beneath Greg's friendly exterior!'

'I, for one.' Leo turned away to pour the drinks.

'Why? Had you met him before?'

'No. But all men possess a primitive streak. Better hidden in some than in others, I'll allow, but there somewhere, ready to raise its ugly head given the right set of circumstances.' He faced her, his eyes mocking. 'I thought you might have learned that early on in your young life—from me.'

Davina's mouth tightened as she took the glass he offered, but she refused to rise to his bait. 'The awkward thing from my point of view is that Greg and I work in the same building.'

'Ignore the whole thing. Pretend it never happened. Ten to one he'll want to resume your relationship as though nothing was wrong.' Leo sat down beside her on the couch, stretching out his long, brown legs.

Davina sipped her drink cautiously. 'No chance of that. I've no intention of seeing him again socially, I assure you. I'd always be on edge, waiting for him to pounce again. Besides,' she added drily, 'he won't want anything more to do with me after tonight. For one thing he's been made to look ridiculous, and for another he won't be in the least interested now he realises I'm not willing to jump into bed with him.'

Leo's face was curious as he turned to look at her. 'Why won't you, Davy? Don't you care for that sort of thing?'

'Sex you mean?'

He blinked. 'Well—yes.'

Davina chuckled. 'I'm perfectly normal, Leo. But I think I'm entitled to wait until *I* want to make love, too. When it's a mutual thing; not something taken for granted as a run-of-the-mill way to round off an evening.' She finished her brandy and yawned. 'Sorry. Must be all the excess emotion tonight. Not to mention the fall on my *derrière.*'

Leo grinned in sympathy and reached out to squeeze her hand. 'Poor Davy. Next time you get swept off your feet I'd recommend someone less likely to drop you.'

'Be fair! Poor Greg *was* trying to fend off Casey.'

'Very true. I'm grateful to Casey.'

Davina turned her head against the sofa cushions, looking at him speculatively. 'Why?'

'I don't like to think of you in distress, Davy, of any kind. I know I caused you a fair amount myself in the past, but it's not a thought that gives me much pleasure, believe me.'

Something in his eyes recalled Davina to the fact that it was high time she returned to her own domain. 'All that's over and done with, Leo. I've recovered from all my youthful passions and agonies long since, believe me, you included.'

'Good. I'm pleased to hear it.'

There was dismissal in his tone and Davina got up at once, feeling rebuffed. 'Thanks for the drink, Leo. I'm sorry you had to be involved in my embarrassing little imbroglio downstairs, but fear not, you won't be troubled by anything similar again.' She moved past him as he rose, but he caught her wrist, halting her.

'Davy,' he said quietly, and turned her round to face him. 'Can't we be friends? Must Madeleine and Sean always stand between us as a barrier?'

Davina's eyes dropped. 'Of course not,' she said lightly. 'But you and I lead very different lives. Very separate, both geographically and socially.'

'I wasn't suggesting we became lovers!' His tone was caustic, and Davina pulled away sharply.

'I didn't imagine you were. I would never have presumed anything so exalted. But if you mean you'd like an annual Christmas card, or whatever, I'm perfectly willing to oblige.'

Leo looked impatient. 'There must be something by way of a medium; some middle course like other people, Davy. Or do your feelings only veer violently towards love or—indifference?'

She shrugged. 'I'm perfectly ordinary, Leo. But you aren't. And that's all I meant. To me you stand for disquiet—purely by association. Sean and Madeleine affect me the same way. And I prefer a quiet life. When you're around my life is anything but, it seems to me.'

'You can hardly blame me for the young knight errant's clumsy attempt at seduction tonight!'

'I don't. But I'm not sure I'm grateful for your intervention, even though you meant well,' she said, with deliberate sweetness. She looked at the scar on his arm. 'Healing well, I see. Good. Now it's time I went— please don't bother to come down. I don't anticipate any further dramas. Goodnight.' Davina ran down the stairs quickly, glad to get away from Leo and his brooding expression as he acknowledged her goodnight.

What an evening, she thought wearily, as she prepared for bed. Why were men so difficult! There was Greg wanting to be her lover, when friendship was all she wanted from him, and Leo asking to be friends when all she wanted . . . Davina stood arrested, hairbrush in hand, and stared at herself in the mirror trying to decide exactly what she did want from Leo.

She crawled into bed, refusing to face up to the truth, which was unpalatable in the extreme. She felt sore in mind and body, and angry. And try as she might to ignore it, a still, small voice in her mind told her very distinctly that she was angry because Leo had said he wasn't suggesting they became lovers. Not that she *wanted* them to be lovers, of course. She was just angry because she would have preferred to be the one who made that particular point clear, not Leo Seymour.

The practice was very busy for the first part of the following week. All the doctors seemed to need countless referral letters to consultants, and Dr Harvey required a very erudite article drafted several times for submission to a medical journal, with the result that after three days spent closeted in her stuffy little office Davina felt cross and anti-social, and for once reluctant to do a spell of late evening duty at reception afterwards. She had agreed to it weeks before to help out during the holiday period, and was heartily sorry by late evening midway through the week. Helen was full of sympathy as they went the rounds together afterwards, locking up.

'I'm done to a frazzle after only an afternoon here, so God knows what you must feel like after a day in the office plus two hours on the desk.'

'Hot and horrible,' said Davina tersely.

'Going out with young Dr Kildare tonight?'

'No. Just a walk with Casey, a long, long soak in the tub, some salad on a tray with a book, then bed.' Davina stretched luxuriously as they emerged into the sunshine of the June evening. 'Sheer bliss.'

Helen looked envious as they strolled through the village together. 'Sounds nice. I've got two little dears to scrub and a basket of ironing in front of me.'

'And a nice, kind husband who will have fed those same little dears *and* done the washing up!'

Helen laughed, acknowledging Davina's inside knowledge of the Bates ménage, and they parted to walk in opposite directions. The heatwave which had begun in time for the church fête had outlasted all predictions, and the evening was very warm. Poor old Casey would be very fed up, thought Davina with guilt, and began to hurry as she turned into Glebe Lane. She always left the small windows in the kitchen open for him, but even so the flat was likely to be very stuffy for the poor old dog.

When she arrived in the back garden of Ivy Cottage Davina found she was wrong on both counts. Casey was not at all fed up, and the ground floor wasn't in the least stuffy. The door and windows were wide open and Casey lay near the rustic seat at the end of the garden, looking perfectly happy. And lounging on the seat were Margaret Lennox and Leo Seymour, with gin and tonics on the small iron table beside them, both of them so deep in conversation neither of them noticed Davina's arrival until Casey dragged himself to his feet to welcome her.

'Darling!' Mrs Lennox jumped up to embrace her daughter, smiling, and Leo rose with her, his eyes wary as Davina looked from her mother's face to his.

'Well, well, where did you spring from?' Davina asked her mother. 'I wasn't expecting you until next week.' She turned to Leo. 'Hello, there. Thanks for entertaining my mother.'

'My pleasure,' he said quietly.

'I *did* ring the practice,' said Mrs Lennox, 'but the girl who answered said you were with one of the doctors so I thought I'd just come straight here, and fortunately met Leo who managed to unlock the door connecting his part of the house to yours.'

Davina looked at Leo, startled. 'Is there a key?'

'No. I picked the lock.'

Making a mental note to get a bolt fixed, Davina sat down in the place vacated by Leo, while he lounged on the grass, propped up on one elbow.

'Sarah's mother came for a visit, so I decided to leave the field clear for her and come to see you,' said Mrs Lennox, examining her daughter's face critically. 'You look very weary, my love.'

'Busy day,' said Davina.

Leo looked at her disapprovingly. 'You work very long hours. Too long. You look worn out.'

'Well, thanks!' Davina's chin lifted. 'You work long hours yourself.'

'Not *all* the time.'

'Ditto. We're short-staffed at the moment, owing to holidays. Things will be back to normal next week.' Davina was annoyed to hear herself justifying her way of life to Leo, and turned back to her mother. 'How long are you staying?'

'I'm not sure.' Mrs Lennox looked from one carefully blank face to the other. 'A day or two perhaps, if you'll have me.'

Davina put her arm round her mother and kissed her lovingly. 'Yes, please. I've missed you.'

'And you could do with a square meal, by the look of you.' Mrs Lennox returned the kiss. 'Let's start right now and go down to that nice pub in the village for dinner. There's not enough to feed a mouse in your kitchen.'

'OK,' said Davina, with only a fleeting regret for her original plan for the evening.

'Will you join us, Leo?' asked Mrs Lennox.

He got to his feet in a swift, graceful movement, smiling in apology. 'Mrs Lennox, there's nothing I'd like better, but I'm afraid it's a working dinner for me tonight. John Wynne Jones is cooking something ominously Celtic at his lodge, and a bunch of us from the unit plan to thrash out a little problem while we eat it. We struck rather a snag today, which is the reason

I'm home early. We decided to pack it in for a time and return to the fray again this evening.'

'Problems?' asked Davina.

Leo sighed. 'Jack's having a spot of difficulty with the girl playing Annabella Milbanke, the woman Byron married. She's supposed to be resistant to him almost to the point of hostility, whereas the fair Briony is altogether too obviously responsive to Jack the lad, which meant take after take today, and she still couldn't get it right. Not his fault, mind. Jack in everyday gear mows the girls down, but in full Byronic rig as the archetypal Regency buck he's too much altogether for poor Briony.'

'So what are you going to do?'

Leo shrugged. 'Jack seems to think he's hit on the answer. I hope to God he's right.'

Over dinner in the Bull later that evening, Margaret Lennox gave Davina a very straight look. 'You didn't tell me Leo had moved into the other part of Ivy Cottage, Davina.'

Davina looked guilty. 'I forgot. Anyway, I don't see him much. He's only here temporarily while he's making this film about Byron.'

'I see.' Mrs Lennox looked thoughtful. 'Odd that Leo should have chosen to resurrect this particular film, isn't it, considering all the brouhaha when the original one was abandoned.'

'I don't imagine the publicity will do any harm, Mother! And it's a bit different this time. Leo's actually **directing it. There's been quite a lot about it in the Press.'**

'So I've noticed. Of course, John Wynne Jones is a much bigger name these days—so is Leo. His films tend to hit the headlines rather, don't they? Such a passion for the controversial!'

'But they're good box office too, which is the important thing. And I gather this one has foreign backing, despite an all-British cast, so Leo doesn't have to worry about running out of money, or actresses running off in the middle.' Davina turned away to examine the temptations of the sweet trolley and missed the worried look on her mother's face.

'Does having Leo around bother you?' asked Mrs Lennox. 'Rake up unpleasant memories from the past, I mean.'

Davina shook her head positively. 'Lord, no. Credit me with more fibre than that!' She grinned reassuringly. 'If I'm not as thrilled as I might be over having Leo as fellow tenant it's probably because of what happened the other night.' She gave her mother an account of Greg's unwanted he-man tactics and her rescue from them, both by Casey and Leo. Mrs Lennox was amused, as Davina intended, but changed her mind about taking Casey back with her.

'I'll feel happier if he stays with you for the time being,' she said firmly.

'Fine.' Davina was only too pleased to have Casey stay with her. 'Then you can take off on your travels whenever you like, without having to come here first all the time.'

'I come here to see *you*, not just to deposit Casey!'

'Yes, I know.' Davina smiled lovingly. 'But in case of emergency, like multiple chicken pox, or something, you're freer to take off at a moment's notice. Now; give me the latest news on all the Lennox babies.'

Nothing loath, Mrs Lennox was only too ready to hold forth on the subject at length, and it was very late by the time she was finally installed in Davina's bed while her daughter made do with the sofa in the parlour. The sofa was small, and fitted even Davina's small dimensions so exactly she found it hard to sleep. The night was hot and sultry and Casey was restless, so after a while Davina put on her dressing-gown and went out into the garden with him. She sat on the seat at the far end near the syringa, drinking in its scent as she leaned back, her fingers stroking Casey's head as she slowly relaxed in the cooler air. After a while she dozed a little, then jerked awake as Casey growled deep in his throat. He quietened again almost at once as he recognised the figure coming across the lawn. Even in the dim starlight, it was unmistakably Leo. There was something in the way he moved, Davina mused sleepily. Her greeting was so friendly for once that Leo was taken aback, she could tell, and she sat up as Leo returned her greeting softly.

'I couldn't sleep,' she said, 'neither could Casey, so we came out here.'

Leo sat down beside her on the seat, close enough for her to feel the warmth from his body through his thin summer clothes. 'I was about to turn on my light when I looked from my window and saw something white glimmering down here. I wondered if you'd left something or——' He halted, then gave an odd little laugh. 'I'm lying. I came down to see if it was you. I hoped it was you.'

'Why?'

'Because I wanted to share something with you, Davy.' He turned to look down at her and she could see his eyes glinting in the starlight as he smiled. 'I thought you'd like to hear Jack's solution to the problem of Briony.'

Davina giggled, and settled herself more comfortably. 'What did he do? Wear a mask during dinner?'

Leo reached over casually and took her hand. 'Not too far out, as it happens.' The actor, it seemed, had decided on his own method of turning off the lady.

When his guests arrived at the lodge Jack greeted them wearing hideous trousers with braces, a sweatshirt with a vulgar slogan across his broad chest, and dark stubble on his unshaved chin. To top it all the small lodge had been redolent with the delicacy Jack assured them had been prepared by his own fair hands.

'Honest to God, Davy,' said Leo, 'it was enough to knock you down the minute you went through the door, and a bit over the top for a hot summer's night.'

The celebrated romantic actor, it seemed, have served his guests highly seasoned faggots, which Jack took some pains to explain were made from pigs' liver in true Welsh style. They were garnished with mounds of fried onions and awash in pints of red-hot gravy, and Jack had tucked into them with all the finesse of a starving animal, washing them down with copious draughts of beer.

'You should have seen him,' went on Leo. 'He picked his teeth, he told filthy jokes, laughed like a drunken hyena most of the time, and Briony just sat there, mute, looking sicker and sicker.'

'Poor girl!'

'Wait—the best is yet to come. After dinner our hero spent the rest of the evening chatting up my assistant, in regrettably amorous fashion.'

Davina whistled softly. 'That must have been the final straw for poor Briony—though your assistant must be pretty tolerant to stand Jack's advances under the circumstances.'

'Oh he is, he is!' Leo spluttered with laughter. 'His name's Mick Doyle, and he and Jack were in college together. As they both took trouble to point out to the unfortunate Briony, they really are *very* old friends.'

'Pigs!' Davina laughed unwillingly. 'So now she thinks Jack's—oh, that's dreadful. Serve him right if she tells the Press.'

'She won't do that,' said Leo with certainty. 'I drove her back to her digs myself, and hinted that if word ever got out the film would fold and her career would never get off the ground. I also hinted that if she did well as Annabella I might cast her in a more important role in my next film.'

'Machiavelli!'

'Not a bit of it—just practical. I'm damned if anything's going to put a damper on the Byron film this time round.'

'Had you any idea beforehand what Jack had in mind?'

'No. I went to the lodge fully prepared to thrash out tomorrow's scenes, nothing more. Jack's performance came as a shock.' Leo shuddered. 'The memory of it—not to mention the meal—is likely to give me nightmares. Though from a purely professional point of view the villain deserves an Oscar.'

They lapsed into comfortables silence while Leo kept her hand in his and Davina stroked Casey with her free one. It was very pleasant to sit alone in a dark garden late at night with Leo Seymour, she found, and smiled at her thought and in some extra-sensory way he knew she was smiling and asked why.

'Oh, Jack, I suppose, and you and me here like Darby and Joan——'

'Not Darby and Joan,' he protested. 'Surely you can think of something more romantic than that!'

'What do you suggest, then, Mr Director?'

'Let me see . . . no balcony, so Romeo and Juliet won't do.'

'*And* we're much too old.'

'True. How about Abelard and Héloise, or Paolo and Francesca, or, considering our propensity for disagreement, perhaps Beatrice and Benedick?'

'A bit more apt than the others,' said Davina, 'since Madeleine was the great love of your life. You certainly made enough fuss when she left you.' She held her breath as she felt him stiffen, then suddenly Leo threw back his head and laughed.

'Oh Davy, Davy—not a girl to mince words, are you!' She bit her lip. 'I didn't mean to hurt—or offend——'

'I know. But I wish you could forget Madeleine as far as I'm concerned, Davy.'

Privately Davina considered the boot was on the other foot, but forbore to say so, rather conscious she had been outspoken enough for one night. 'It's time I went in,' she said, and tried to draw away, but Leo kept a firm hold on her hand.

'Stay a few minutes longer,' he said softly, and Davina's resistance, lower than usual in the warm, scented darkness, fell to the level where she yielded when Leo slid an arm round her waist and drew her head down to his shoulder with disarming gentleness. She lay quietly against his shoulder for a long, dreamy interval, until it seemed only natural that Leo should bring the interlude to an end by tilting her chin so that he could kiss her mouth. Davina stopped breathing as Leo's first gentleness gave way almost at once to urgency. She could feel his heart thudding against her, then he gasped, and Davina jerked away involuntarily, averting her head.

'What is it?' he demanded in an urgent whisper. 'Did I hurt you?'

'N—no,' stammered Davina embarrassed, and to her relief Casey woke up and nosed between them, relieving the tension.

'I assume I was too precipitate,' said Leo, each syllable very precise as he rose to his feet and helped her up.

'Something like that.' Davina clicked her fingers to Casey, who padded slowly behind them to the house as they strolled down the garden.

'Are you always so difficult when it comes to making love?' asked Leo caustically. 'I was an eye-witness to your response to your young doctor the other night. And now I've got first-hand experience of it myself. Yet I could have sworn that for a moment there you felt the same way as me.'

As they reached the cottage Davina made herself face Leo in the light coming from her kitchen window. 'I did,' she whispered, not wanting to wake her mother. 'Only—I don't think you'll be amused this time if I'm blunt about what turned me off.'

'Possibly not, but I'm not going until I find out.' He took her by the shoulders and shook her gently. 'Tell me, Davy. What did I do wrong?'

She stared at him unhappily, then sighed. 'To be painfully frank, Leo, you ate too many of Jack's fried onions.'

CHAPTER SIX

'NO SIGN of Leo since yesterday evening,' remarked Mrs Lennox, while she served what she described as 'a proper meal' at dinner the following evening.

'Busy with his beloved film,' said Davina, mouth full, and changed the subject. Mrs Lennox took the hint and announced that the laundry was done, the kitchen cupboards and the refrigerator contained real food, and the flat had been cleaned to within an inch of its life. As this last had been glaringly apparent the moment Davina arrived home, she thanked her mother meekly on all counts, and apologised for having left her to her own devices all day.

'Not my devices—yours,' said Mrs Lennox with severity. 'I wish you'd look after yourself a little better. I suspect you rarely eat enough, and devoutly hope it's not some quirky idea about dieting.'

'No, Mother.'

'And look at the time! Seven at night is too late to get home from the practice. You work too hard.'

'Yes, Mother.'

Margaret Lennox eyed her meek daughter with suspicion. 'Not short of money, are you?'

'No, Mother.'

'Trouble with the opposite sex?'

'No, Mother.'

Mrs Lennox gave up, and spent the rest of the evening doing a bit of mending on various items in Davina's wardrobe. 'I'm off in the morning,' she said as they went to bed. 'As soon as you can get some time off come down to Surrey. You need a change and a rest.'

Davina missed her mother very much after only two

71

days of her company, but since the rest of the week continued hectic, had little inclination in the evenings to do more that eat, bathe and fall into bed after exercising Casey. Of Leo there was no sign, apart from a few footsteps overhead late at night. Davina felt unexpectedly depressed about it, sorry she had been so candid, and spent quite a lot of time wondering if she was abnormal when it came to the urges of the flesh. Surely one was supposed to be lost to everything else in the world in a lover's arms, not turned off quite sharply by the merest whiff of John Wynne Jone's culinary efforts.

Shortly after she was in bed one night, Davina stiffened at the unmistakable sound of feminine laughter, and went hot all over at the realisation that Leo had someone in his flat. A female someone. It was too warm to pull the covers over her head to block out the faint sounds of music and voices, and Davina lay rigid, bristling with a variety of emotions: disgust, anger, and—jealousy, she realised suddenly, and heaved herself over in bed to switch on her radio, turning up the volume to drown out the sound-effects coming from upstairs. It seemed like hours before she heard a car drive away and all was quiet once more.

If only she could move, she thought with passion. The prospect of listening to Leo's little orgies night after night was unbearable. She thumped her pillow viciously, thankful the next day was Saturday and she could stay in bed in the morning. Unfortunately Casey had very different ideas and had her up at first light, begging to be let out, which was unusual. She leaned yawning in the doorway as the dog plodded slowly down the garden to his favourite tree. Suddenly Leo's voice sounded quietly from overhead.

'Davy—are you there?'

Davina retreated stealthily into the kitchen, her hackles rising at the sound of his voice. Unfortunately

Casey, who couldn't see anything a foot away from his nose, had retained his aural powers intact, and came back down the garden as fast as his old joints allowed, wagging his tail as he looked up myopically towards the sound of the familiar voice.

'Hello, old fellow. Where's your boss?' asked Leo.

Out of sight, thought Davina, willing the dog to come in. Casey stayed where he was, and with a sigh of frustration she went back to bed, leaving the door ajar for Casey to follow in his own good time. A little later she heard Leo's car start up and purr away and relaxed, then Casey's tongue wiped her face and with a grunt the dog settled down beside her bed and Davina went back to sleep. When she woke her Saturday was half over, and with a rush she dressed and went off to the tennis club. A cricket match was in progress on the adjoining pitch, and when the day's various matches were over the bar was lively with triumphant, thirsty cricketers in addition to the usual tennis crowd, and when some of them suggested a meal down at the Bull, asking Davina and a few of the other girls to join them, she dashed home to shower and change and feed Casey. He plodded round the garden very slowly, as usual, but ignored his dinner, and after a few mouthfuls of water returned to his bed.

Davina spent a noisy, cheerful evening, but felt uneasy about Casey, and went home earlier than usual to check on him. As she walked briskly down Glebe Lane she saw Leo's car standing outside Ivy Cottage and eyed it with hostility as she opened the gate, wondering if Leo had company again. Then thunder rumbled in the distance and she forgot about Leo in her efforts to unlock her door quickly. Poor Casey hated thunder. For once he made no effort to get out of his bed to greet her, and his dinner was still untouched. As Davina went down on her knees beside him his tail wagged very feebly and her throat constricted as she looked at him more closely. Something was very wrong. The old dog was panting, his breath wheezing alarmingly in his chest, and his nose was hot. His eyes were dull and half closed and Davina stroked him in anguish.

'Casey, what is it? What can I do for you?' She jumped to her feet, running for the telephone, then halted, her mind blank on the subject of vets. Casey had only come for visits. He had never needed a vet until now. Yellow Pages, she thought feverishly, and tried to think what she had done with the directory, which was nowhere to be found. Leo! He might have one. She ran to the connecting door and tried the knob, almost sobbing with relief as it turned and the door opened.

'Leo!' she called up the stairs. 'Leo, it's Davina, can you help me please?'

Leo appeared instantly, leaping down the stairs two at a time. 'What is it?' he demanded.

'Casey—he's ill.'

Leo ran ahead of her to the kitchen, and bent over the dog, his hand gentle on the animal's head. He turned to look up at Davina's distraught face. 'We'd better get him to a vet.'

'I don't know which one is nearest,' she said thickly. 'I couldn't find——'

'Ring the operator. Here—I'll do it.'

Within minutes Leo had located a vet, explained the problem and returned to Davina, who was crouched down by the dog, feverishly murmuring comfort in his ear.

'Found one a couple of miles away,' said Leo briefly. 'Let's get Casey in the car.'

Davina stared up at him. 'Can't the vet come here?'

Leo raised her gently to her feet. 'He advises us to take Casey there, where all the necessary equipment's on hand for whatever's wrong with the poor old chap. Come on, Davy. Give me a hand.'

He tossed his car-keys to her and told her to unlock the car and spread out the travelling rug on the back seat. He heaved the groaning animal up in his arms and followed Davina's flying figure down the path, and a few moments later Casey was installed in the back seat of the car with his head on Davina's lap while Leo broke the speed limit along empty country lanes.

Barely half an hour later they were on the way back home, Davina weeping silently as Leo drove more slowly this time, making no attempt to offer unwanted consolation, wisely letting her cry. When they arrived at the cottage he led her straight upstairs to his own rooms, installed her on the sofa and, still without speaking, poured brandy into two glasses and handed her one. Davina drank obediently while Leo swallowed his own brandy in one draught. Then he sat down beside her, drew her on to his lap and turned her face into his shoulder, smoothing her hair in wordless sympathy. They stayed where they were until Davina's tears ran dry, and eventually she drew away a little, pushing at her hair as she looked up into Leo's face. His ruler-straight brows drew together as he met her look.

'You knew, didn't you?' she asked hoarsely.

He sighed deeply. 'Yes, Davy, I knew. One look at the poor old fellow was enough. That's why I insisted on taking you to the vet instead of vice versa.'

Davina nodded sadly. 'That's what you meant by the necessary equipment. You knew he'd have to be put down.' She looked about her vaguely. 'Time I went, I think.'

Leo set her gently on her feet. 'Stay here for a moment while I check everything's all right downstairs. We took off without locking either of your doors.'

Davina hardly noticed him go. She sat limply in a corner of the sofa, trying to frame the words of her telephone call to her mother, hating the very thought of breaking the news.

When Leo returned he refused to let her go without a cup of tea. 'You need a hot drink,' he said firmly, and since nothing in the world seemed worth argument for the moment Davina obediently drank the tea he made for her, but refused offers of food.

'Have you had dinner tonight?' he demanded.

'Yes. Down at the Bull.' It seemed like days since her cheerful, lively evening, instead of mere hours. Casey had still been alive then—Davina clamped down on the thought and got up. 'I really must be off, now, Leo. I can't thank you enough for——'

A deafening clap of thunder drowned the rest of her words, and lightning lit up the room. The threatening storm had finally broken. Leo pulled her into his arms as she flinched.

'Afraid of storms, Davy?'

'No. Casey was, though. At least he's missed this one.' Her voice wavered and Leo cradled her against him.

'Oh, Davy . . .'

His tenderness almost ruined her precarious self-control, and Davina broke free. 'You'll have me howling again if you don't stop being so kind, Leo Seymour.' She smiled shakily at his troubled face. 'Thank you. I don't know what I'd have done without you.'

'You'd have coped, Davy. But I'm glad you called on me for help.'

The storm was very noisy as Leo saw Davina safely downstairs to her own flat. 'We ought to do something about that,' he said, nodding at the communicating door.

Davina flushed. 'Sorry I barged through like that. You could have been having a party, or something.'

'I wasn't. Not even "something".' His eyes laughed at her. 'I regard this place as a bolthole where I can shut myself off from the film world. Admittedly I brought the Delaneys back for a drink the other night, but only because a few problems needed ironing out. But *you* can use the door any time you like, Davy. I promise I won't make free with it myself. Bolt it your side if you prefer. Goodnight.'

As Davina prepared for bed, she was rather guilty to find her sorrow over Casey mitigated just very slightly by the fact that Leo's guests the other evening had been the female star of his film and her husband. No orgy after all. Even so, in view of the storm and her grief Davina was pessimistic about her chances of sleep, and prepared for a bad night. Instead, utterly drained by grief, she slept more heavily than usual, and woke only because someone was hammering on the connecting door.

'Wake up, Davy,' Leo called loudly.

Heavy-eyed and depressed, she pulled on her dressing-gown and let him in, feeling even worse at the sight of him since Leo was obviously showered and shaved and looked businesslike in checked shirt, blue sweater and jeans.

'Come on,' he said briskly. 'I'm taking you out for the day.'

Davina stared at him, the events of the previous night flooding back. No Casey to take outside this morning. No wagging tale and short-sighted canine eyes to look up at her with devotion. The eyes regarding her at the moment were understanding, but impersonal, as though Leo had done all the comforting he was going to do. 'But it's raining cats and dogs——' She swallowed, then started again. 'It's a terrible day, Leo. Where on earth would we go in this downpour?'

'To Hadfield Chase. You went there with me once before, remember?'

'How could I forget? But why would I want to go again?'

'Because if you stay home here on your own you'll

grieve over Casey. I'm going to work, so I suggest you come with me and watch Lord Byron toying with the forbidden delights of bedding his half-sister Augusta.'

Davina brightened. 'You mean it?'

'Of course I do,' he said impatiently. 'Come *on*, Davy, time's a-wasting. I'll give you ten minutes in the bathroom while I make you some coffee, then we're off.'

When they were in the sleek comfort of the Jaguar Davina remembered guiltily that she hadn't rung her mother, and realised she now knew why Leo had insisted on looking through her flat before she went down to it the night before. He had taken the trouble to get rid of everything of Casey's. She had no idea where everything had gone, but bowls, bed and bedding were missing, and she thanked him for his thoughtfulness.

'I'm really quite a nice sort of chap,' he said, peering through the wall of rain, 'if only you'd admit it.'

'Oh, I do,' she assured him. 'If only——'

'Life's too short for "if onlys",' he cut in. 'Hold on, we're at the lodge. I'm picking up Jack this morning.'

John Wynne Jones looked haggard in the early morning gloom as he dived into the back of the car. He cheered up as he saw Davina. 'Hell*o*, how are you? Come to watch the fun today? Morning, Leo,' he added belatedly. 'God-awful day.'

'Perfect for indoor scenes, old son.' Leo grinned at the actor and reversed out into the road. 'I trust you're feeling sufficiently decadent today, Jack. I want this particular scene in the can today.'

'If the censor ever passes it,' retorted the Welshman gloomily. 'I just hope I'm not expending my considerable expertise and enormous talent on something likely to end up on the cutting-room floor!'

'Is it so very naughty then?' asked Davina curiously.

Jack leaned on the back of her seat and leered at her. 'It's not so much what we *do*, darling, as what we imply we're *about* to do. You must have seen Leo's stuff. Much too subtle for heaving bare bodies and all that huffing and puffing that goes on in less artistic pieces.'

'Lay off, Jack,' said Leo irritably. 'Keep your energy for the job. Remember I want it *right* today. Yesterday you were somewhere else as far as I could judge.'

'Blame the weather. Can't stand storms—feel 'em in my blood before they come.'

Leo muttered something uncomplimentary about melodramatic Welsh idiots, and Jack winked at Davina. 'I don't know that I'll be much better today, mind, a good chapel man like me. My conscience says I shouldn't be making love to anyone on the Sabbath.'

'Tell your conscience you're being paid for it—overpaid, even. That should shut it up.' Leo turned the car through the entrance to Hadfield Chase, where the whole place was already pulsing with life. The gardens were a closely packed encampment of caravans, props wagons and generators, with people rushing about everywhere, and the house itself, Davina saw, as Leo took her on a swift tour, was transformed. Slabs of polystyrene filled out fallen walls and formed false arches among the ruins, and inside, holes had been cut in ceilings to let in arc-lights in some of the rooms, which were furnished in early nineteenth-century style: a dining-room with oval gate-legged table and graceful chairs upholstered in striped satin, a bedroom with four-poster bed under a tent-like canopy of fringed silk.

'Facsimile of the bed he put "to uses vile",' murmured Leo.

Davina smiled at him in excitement. She inspected everything in detail, acknowledged brief introductions to people dashing about in apparent confusion, which at some stage suddenly resolved itself. A chair was placed for Davina alongside Leo, who had a brief word with the continuity girl behind him, then John Wynne Jones and Joanna Delaney took their places at the table, which was laid for a dinner already consumed, wine at low levels in the goblets, candles flickering in triple-branched candelabra.

Davina watched, enthralled, hardly able to recognise Jack, the flippant Welshman of the car-ride, in the black-clad Regency buck with eyes smouldering in his face, which was made up to look 'hellishly pale' in true Byronic fashion under the clustering black curls above his brow. Opposite him sat Joanna, also transformed, in a low-cut velvet gown and a wig with clusters of ringlets over each ear.

'Right,' called out Leo. 'Let's go.'

'Positions!' yelled an acolyte, and Leo issued brief instructions to his actors.

'Silence!' bawled Leo's assistant, and John Wynne Jones lolled in his seat, smiling at Joanna with a suppressed, burning excitement Davina could almost feel. Joanna seemed to mirror his emotion in her huge brilliant eyes, laughing with him, teasing and artful, complicity in every line of her beautiful face and body, as a camera tracked slowly backwards, a press photo-grapher clicked away rapidly in the background, then Leo said coolly,

'Good. Cut.'

At once George Gordon, sixth Lord Byron, changed back into John Wynne Jones. 'How was that, Leo?' he called, like a small boy asking praise for his homework.

'Good. OK.'

Leo didn't believe in superlatives, thought Davina, amused. And he had obviously forgotten she was there as he went over to his principal actors and went into a huddle with them.

'Now remember, Jack,' he said as he returned to his chair. 'Augusta's the one woman who, according to Byron, neither deceived nor forsook him. But don't forget. She's forbidden fruit!'

Jack rolled his eyes. 'There's lovely. Come on then, Jo—let's at it.'

And once again the process was repeated, and again and again until Leo was finally satisfied. Eventually he turned to Davina with a tired grin, no longer the absorbed director but the man she knew, or at least thought she knew. This gifted, relentless man was quite a revelation. Seeing him at work added new dimensions to the Leo Seymour who lived in the upper-floor flat of Ivy Cottage. Not sure whether she was happy at the thought Davina smiled back at him shyly.

'That was utterly fascinating. Thanks for bringing me.'

'Can you bear to stay all day, Davy? I'd like to finish this particular sequence if humanly possible.'

Davina was perfectly happy to stay indefinitely. She enjoyed everything in this different, exotic world, even the endless coffee from plastic cups, not minding in the least when the conversation going on around her was as esoteric as another language. At times Leo would remember she was there and break off to explain some particularly mystifying bit of jargon, or ask if she were bored, but Davina was able to assure him with complete truth that she was having the time of her life. The actors were a friendly crowd, including the beautiful Joanna Delaney, also the unfortunate Briony, a very attractive dark girl who quite obviously couldn't stand Jack anywhere near her.

'Awkward for the later scenes,' murmured Leo under his breath to Davina. 'By all accounts Annabella Milbanke quite enjoyed her year of conjugal bliss with Byron before she renounced him and his evil ways. If poor Briony finds Jack's embraces so abhorrent I might have to cut her part drastically.'

'Pigs—both of you!' hissed Davina in his ear.

Leo grinned. 'I don't suppose you'd volunteer to let Jack chat you up a bit—sort of reassure the poor girl?' He stopped, frowning. 'No, on second thoughts, don't bother. Jack's too bloody good at the chatting up.' He looked very deliberately into her eyes. 'As far as anything of that sort is concerned, Davina Lennox, I would very much prefer you stick to me.'

Davina flushed scarlet, but there was no opportunity to reply as the next session of shooting was about to begin, and went on for so long even Davina's enthusiasm began to flag. She was very glad when Leo called it a day at last, though rather surprised to find herself alone with him in the car on the return journey. Jack, it seemed, was getting a lift back with some of the technicians, and was off to the local pub.

'I didn't think you could stick another session of shop-talk over pints of bitter,' said Leo casually. 'How about a meal at the Blue Boar on the way back?'

Davina looked down at herself doubtfully. 'I'm not dressed for anything special, Leo.'

'Pretty much the same as me,' he pointed out.

Davina took a few minutes in the cloakroom when they reached the Blue Boar, sorry she was wearing nothing more exciting than a pink cotton sweater and denims, but since Leo was unconcerned she shrugged philosophically, brushed her hair, put on some lipstick and went off to join him. He was in the bar, leaning against it as he chatted to the landlord. Davina could see two young girls at a nearby table completely ignoring their male companions while they excitedly discussed the tall, tawny-haired man, and debated hotly on his identity. Davina went past them as slowly as she could, unashamedly eavesdropping. Conscious of a new proprietorial feeling, she joined Leo, very much aware that the two pretty young faces were turned enviously in her direction.

'You're attracting some attention,' she told him. 'The ladies behind us fancy they've seen you before.'

Leo glanced across at the girls and smiled, and they bridled and blushed, and their boyfriends scowled. 'Probably seen a photograph somewhere,' he said casually. 'Come on, let's go through into the dining-room. The landlord says we can have it to ourselves. He doesn't serve food on Sunday nights.'

'Then let me cook you something at home——'

'He's serving food to *us*, Davy.' Leo smiled indulgently. 'I ordered it this morning.'

'Cheat!' Davina laughed as they were shown to a table in the small, deserted dining-room. 'Pity we're on our own in here, though,' she whispered as the landlord went away. 'I was rather enjoying the reflected glory.'

'While I infinitely prefer to have you to myself, after a hard day behind the camera. Tell me: what did you think of the bit you saw?'

Davina was able to say, with complete honesty, that she thought it brilliant. While they waited for the food they discussed the day's shooting and Leo answered the barrage of questions Davina put to him so eagerly, clearly gratified she found it all so interesting.

'I was afraid you'd get bored once the novelty wore off.'

'Bored!' Davina shook her head vigorously. 'How could anyone be bored while all that was going on? Besides, it's given me so much of an insight into how it's done.'

They ate roast beef with all the trimmings and talked non-stop, not only about the film in production, but about Leo's next venture, which was to be a psychological thriller centring on a murder trial. Then he firmly changed the subject to her own work, and asked about life at the practice, showing rather pointed interest in her social life. Davina was happy to tell him anything he wanted to know, and it was late by the time they left the inn.

Leo apologised as he opened the car door for her. 'You'll be tired in the morning.'

'It was worth it. I've had a lovely day.' She smiled at him warmly as he slid in beside her. 'I know you did it to take my mind off poor old Casey, and I appreciate it very much, Leo.'

He turned to look at her, one eyebrow raised. 'I think I should make it clear I'm not quite as altruistic as all that, Davy. Part of my motive was to get you out of the house and stop you grieving, admittedly, but it *was* only part. The rest of it was a subtle ploy to enjoy your company for a whole day.' He started the car and Davina sat back, not sure what to make of his statement. She glanced at his profile, frowning. Did he mean it?

'Yes, I mean it,' he said, startling her, and she laughed.

'Do you read everyone's mind so easily, Mr Seymour?'

'No. But then, I'm not so interested in other people's minds.'

'Why mine?'

Leo concentrated on the road in silence. 'Because I'd like us to be—friends, Davy,' he said at last.

Friends. Davina thought about it. Was that all he wanted? It sounded surprisingly insipid and unsatisfactory.

'No—that's not really what I mean,' he said, surprising her again. 'But I'm wary of using the actual word I have in mind.'

Feeling absurdly pleased Davina relaxed in the seat as Leo drove the powerful car with controlled skill through the winding, cross-country lanes. 'I was afraid you were permanently offended after my—well, my outspoken little comment the other night.'

He chuckled. 'It took me days to get over it, believe me. No one's ever complained of anything similar before. I should have stopped to brush my teeth before rushing down to see you in the garden, I suppose.'

'I don't think it would have done much good. Jack's onions seemed singularly ferocious!'

Leo shuddered. 'I never want to eat or smell one again. You may have noticed tonight's menu was totally innocent of the wretched things?'

'Why? Do you intend to have another shot at seducing me tonight?' The words were out before Davina had time to think, and she peered at him in consternation as he brought the car to a halt outside Ivy Cottage. His answering smile did nothing to reassure her.

'Your habit of candour will get you into deep trouble one day, young lady. For your information, I hadn't intended any such thing. But now you've put the idea into my head I must say I find it rather tempting.'

Davina slid out of the car and frankly fled up the path to open the door. Leo strolled after her, grinning from ear to ear as he saw her face when she switched on the lights.

'Don't worry, Davy. I promise I shan't try any strong-arm stuff. Just give me one little kiss and I'll go off to my own celibate bed like a lamb.'

To Davina he looked more lion than lamb. The light from her rose-shaded lamps made his hair shine redly, and his eyes were dancing as he stood in the middle of her small parlour, his thumbs hooked in his belt-loops.

'One kiss?' she said suspiciously.

He nodded. 'One solitary, harmless kiss, Davy. But *you* must kiss *me* for being such a kind, nice friend.'

He looked so absurdly smug she giggled suddenly, stood on tip-toe, her hands on his forearms to steady herself as she aimed for his mouth. He made no move to help her, standing erect with no inclination of his head.

'You might co-operate a little!' she scolded.

'What would you like me to do?'

'You know very well. I can't even reach your mouth like this, you rotter.'

Leo obligingly put his hands under her elbows, raising her off her feet so that she dangled with her eyes on level with his. Davina gave him a quick peck on his lips and grinned at him.

'There. You can put me down now.'

'I don't know that I want to.'

Davina kicked him lightly on the shin and Leo howled and put her down with a bump. 'You fight dirty,' he complained. 'Kicking me, whacking my injured arm——'

'Oh, I forgot. How *is* your arm?'

'Very well now, in spite of your attentions.'

Davina shrugged, unrepentant. 'Sorry, but I'm used to defending myself. I grew up with three older brothers, remember . . .' She halted, her smile fading, and Leo took her gently by the shoulders.

'It's all right, Davy. You don't have to watch every word you say with me, you know. That way we'll never establish any kind of relationship.'

Davina's eyes were very steady as they held his. 'Exactly what kind of relationship did you have in mind?'

'This kind.' And Leo bent and kissed her. This time there was only the scent of expensive soap and clean, healthy male, and Davina breathed in with pleasure, her body responding with such spontaneity that Leo tightened his arms round her and coaxed her lips apart. After a while he raised his head to stare down into her brilliant eyes, the angles of his face sharpened by a look she had seen only once before, but recognised with sudden intense excitement. Leo wanted her. She could feel how much by the way his hands shook as they held her.

'I asked for one kiss,' Leo said unsteadily, and Davina smiled.

'Then it's time we said goodnight. Or would you like some coffee?'

Leo's grasp tightened. 'No, I don't want any coffee, Davy. I don't want to say goodnight, either.'

A shiver went through her body, and Davina bit her lip, looking at him uncertainly. 'Are you asking to sleep with me?'

He dropped his arms and stepped back, his eyes hooded. 'I suppose I am—though I'd prefer a spontaneous happening to a discussion on it.'

'I like to get things clear.' Davina was in command of her emotions once more. 'My original experience with you rather tends to make me wary, I suppose, in more ways than one.'

Leo frowned. 'Perhaps I will have that coffee after all, while you explain exactly what you mean.'

Davina went to fill the kettle, while Leo let himself down on the sofa in the parlour. Through the open door she could see he looked rather tired; even a little depressed as he picked up her unopened Sunday newspaper, and she felt guilty. He had been very kind the night before, she reminded herself, and had taken her out to watch the day's shooting today, by no means a run-of-the-mill experience, yet her only thanks had taken the form of a second rebuff the moment he had attempted to make love to her. Which was very stupid, since she *wanted* him to make love to her. She scowled, impatient with herself as she filled two mugs and went over to Leo to sit beside him.

'I suppose it was going back to Hadfield Chase today,' she said with a sigh. 'I couldn't help thinking of the first time I went there with you.'

Leo's eyes took on an absent, remembering look. 'Yes, of course. I took you over there for the day. We played darts in the pub and went for a walk afterwards.'

Her day out with Leo had been an unforgettable experience for the young Davy Lennox. From the moment she was tucked into his elderly Triumph Spitfire sports-car there was an indefinable glamour about the entire occasion. It was only a ten-mile journey to Hadfield Chase, but Davina wished it was longer, sorry when the drive came to an end. Cheeks flushed with cold, her eyes sparkling, she listened, rapt, as Leo took her from room to room in the old ruined house and explained how parts of it would be reconstructed for the film.

'You'll be able to see for yourself when we start shooting.' Leo's face blazed with enthusiasm, plus a controlled, tense sort of elation Davina viewed with wonder. 'The rest of the cast and crew are due back from location today. I came on ahead to sort this place out.'

Afterwards he took her to the local pub and they sat on a hard wooden settle in the public bar, ate bread and cheese and pickles, and drank lager, and after lunch Davina surprised Leo with her skill at darts. When they left the pub later she wondered if that was it, the end of her treat, but Leo soon put her mind at rest.

'Let's find a public footpath and walk, Davy, shall we? I need to burn off some excess energy.'

She agreed rapturously, stealing a glance at his profile as they walked. He was very obviously right about the energy. She could see it in the set of his wide mouth, the occasional flare of his nostrils. Even his hair seemed to crackle with it. He put her in mind of the thoroughbred chestnut at the local stables; always champing at the bit.

They found a footpath which wound up steeply to the crown of a hill with a view of a fair bit of Gloucestershire, and they rested briefly at the top, leaning against a cluster of boulders as they watched the sun slide down the sky in a blaze of vermilion.

'I'd like to capture that on film,' murmured Leo, and his hand tightened on Davina's. 'Quite a spectacle, isn't it, poppet?'

She agreed rapturously, smiling up at him. 'Thank you so much for today, Leo. It's been perfect.'

His eyes warmed as he looked down into her flushed,

happy face. 'I don't need thanks, Davy. The pleasure was entirely mutual . . .' He hesitated, as if to say something else, then changed his mind. Instead he bent his head and kissed her, very gently, on her mouth. Davina's eyes shut tight and her heart missed a beat, then resumed with a heavy, rhythmic thud, almost deafening her as Leo drew away. Her eyes flew open and she clenched her fists to stop her hands from going out to pull him back to her, to make him kiss her again. But the moment was over for Leo. Inexperienced as she was, Davina knew that for him the kiss had been a mere token of appreciation of their day together, nothing remotely resembling the momentous happening it had been for her.

Davina came back to the present with a jolt, aware that Leo was watching her expectantly, waiting for her to speak.

'You sort of—simmered all day,' she said slowly, 'as though the slightest spark would ignite you into some kind of conflagration. Of course I had no idea why you were so keyed up. I only knew you were the most wonderful thing that had ever happened to me.'

'What did I do to alter your opinion, Davy? It must have been something pretty bad for you to remember it so precisely.'

'I'd never fallen in love before. Arrested develop ment, I suppose. But one look at you was enough to change all that. Then, after that wonderful day at Hadfield Chase, you let me into the secret. The thing that had you ticking like a time-bomb all day. You'd just been passing the hours with poor dumb little Davy until it was time to meet Madeleine's train.' Davina smiled at him bleakly. 'I had actually imagined, you see, in my youthful innocence, that you were so—so electric because you were enjoying *my* company, while all the time I was just a stop-gap until the fair Madeleine was restored to your arms.'

All the life drained from Leo's face, and he pushed back his hair, looking defeated. 'So that's the real barrier between us. Not Sean and Madeleine's behaviour at all. The damage was done before they even met, as far as you're concerned.'

'Yes, in a way. Not that I didn't loathe all the rest of it.' Davina looked away. 'But the real hurt was because you never saw me as anything but Sean's rather nice little sister—until Sean took off with your lady. And then for some reason you turned your attentions to me that last night in a way that fairly ravished my adolescent soul.'

Leo slumped back against the sofa cushions. He rubbed a hand wearily over his eyes, then turned to look at her. 'I'm not proud of that bit, believe me. I despised myself afterwards, and what was worse, I couldn't forget——' He stopped abruptly, looking away.

'Forget what?' Leo was silent so long Davina thought he wasn't going to answer.

'You must make allowances,' he said at last, 'for the fact that I wasn't exactly myself at the time. Perhaps that explains why, although I was insane with jealousy over Madeleine, I could still come near to losing my head over you. And you were so young, so obviously untouched—my God, is it any wonder I've always felt so mixed up about you? I was genuinely fond of you, Davy, and *not* just because you were Sean's sister. But I felt so bloody guilty about the way I'd treated you I tried to forget you existed. Until now.'

Davina's heart began to pound. 'And does the thought of me still bother you?' she asked delicately.

He turned sardonic eyes on her. 'Oh, yes, Davy. Since the day of the fête I'm a prey to sleepless nights once more on your behalf. But in a very different way. Now it's as though we'd never met before. You're a beautiful, adult woman, and I'm a man who wants——' He stopped, his face tense. 'You know damn well what I want, Davy.'

'I've got a fair idea.'

'Then instead of discussing what *I* want perhaps you'd care to enlighten me as to your wishes as far as I'm concerned—always assuming you have any, of course.'

Davina faced him squarely. 'My main wish is not to get hurt. Simple as that. If I fall in love with you all over again I might find it hard to glue myself together a second time.'

'Why should you be hurt?' Leo drew her across the space between them until she was in his arms. 'I wouldn't intentionally hurt any woman. Surely you must know that.'

'You didn't intend hurting me all those years ago, but you did.' She stared up into his eyes, her heart beginning to thud against her ribs. 'Oh, Leo— please——'

'Please what?' he murmured, and put the palm of his hand on the place where her heart was beating. 'See? You aren't entirely indifferent to me, are you? I can feel your heart—and your pulse.' He pressed his lips to her wrist, still holding her eyes with his. 'Can you really say with honesty you don't want this?'

Davina shook her head slowly and he bent to kiss her, taking full possession of her mouth, making it clear the time for talking was over. His lips grew more urgent with each heartbeat, his tongue sudden and startling in its entry into her mouth, as if intent on emphasis that he was in command, that this time there would be no rebuff from her for any reason. She had no will left to stop him. The drift of his hands over her skin was a seduction in itself, and she sat up obediently as he pulled her sweater over her head and dealt efficiently with the scrap of satin beneath it. Colour ran high in her face as he gazed at the curves he held cupped in his hands. His breathing quickened, and she gasped as he bent suddenly to kiss her upthrust breasts, his tongue encircling each erectile tip. Davina gritted her teeth together, electrified by the hot whiplash of sensation sparked off by his touch, then Leo drew away, pulling off his shirt and sweater in one great heave, hurling them across the room before pulling her against him so that her breasts were flattened against his chest. It was smooth and hard to the touch and she shivered, at the mercy of her own senses, as Leo slid his fingers down her spine, seeking out each separate vertebra in turn as he kissed her with mounting demand, his other hand sliding into her hair to caress the tender place behind her ear. His mouth left hers to roam along her jaw until it reached her ear, where his tongue flickered over the sensitive whorls inside until she gasped and pleaded, not sure what it was she yearned for until he laughed deep in his throat and closed her parted lips with his.

The shrill of the telephone was sudden and obscene in its intrusion and Davina cried out in protest, her eyes squeezed shut in frustration as Leo raised his head, holding her so tightly his arms threatened to crack her ribs.

'Don't answer it,' he muttered urgently. 'Davy— don't go away!'

'I must. Please—it's late, it might be something urgent.'

In an agony of embarrassment Davina scrambled to her feet and fled to the phone, her back to Leo.

'Davina?' asked her mother. 'Where have you been? I've been trying to get you all day.'

'Hello, Mother.' Davina threw an anguished look over her shoulder at Leo, who was buttoning his shirt. 'Sorry—I've been out. Leo took me to watch a day's shooting on the film.'

'Oh, I see. That was nice.' Mrs Lennox sounded mollified.

Davina swallowed hard. 'Mother, I'm afraid I've got some bad news. It's Casey—he was very ill. The vet had to put him down.'

The next few minutes were fraught with a variety of emotions as Davina told her sad little tale, and while she was telling it Leo came behind her and drew her hard against him. She gave him a startled glance over her shoulder, and breathed in deeply. 'Leo was so good,' she said, and gasped as his fingers found her breasts. 'He—he—took me out for the day—so I—I wouldn't brood——'

'Now stop crying, Davina,' said Mrs Lennox gruffly. 'Casey was very old, and though I'm deeply sorry you had to cope with all that, it was inevitable at his age. Thank God Leo was there.'

'Yes,' agreed Davina in a strangled voice. 'He's been—quite wonderful.'

'You sound terribly upset. Go to bed, darling, and try not to dwell on it.'

The moment Davina put down the phone Leo spun her round in his arms and kissed her hard.

'That wasn't fair,' she said breathlessly when her mouth was free.

Leo grinned unrepentantly. 'I just couldn't resist the temptation. And you must admit it dried your tears.'

'True!' She giggled as she leaned against him, then yawned suddenly. 'I suppose I'd better go to bed.'

'And I, to my everlasting credit, am going to let you.' He laughed softly. 'I think you can say you were saved by the bell, Davy—very literally.'

Her eyes met his candidly. 'I didn't want to be.'

'I know. It's the only consolation I'll take to my solitary couch upstairs.' He sighed theatrically, then his eyes kindled as they dropped to her breasts. 'Kindly cover yourself, Miss Lennox. Or I don't know that I'll be answerable for the consequences.'

She flushed and hurriedly pulled on her sweater, but

his eyes remained fixed at the spot where her nipples showed clearly through the pink cotton and her colour flamed higher. 'Stop looking at me like that, Leo Seymour, it's unsettling. You're a dangerous man—what is it? What have I said?'

'Only that you've more or less hit on the title of the film. It's Lady Caroline Lamb's all too prophetic opinion of Byron before they'd even met—that he was "mad, bad and dangerous to know".' Leo touched his fingers to her cheek, his eyes holding hers very deliberately. 'But *I'm* not any of those things, Davy, I promise.'

Her luminous smile was tinged with mockery. 'You're definitely not mad, and I don't think you're bad, but I reserve judgement on the last!'

CHAPTER SEVEN

JUST how much danger Leo Seymour represented occupied Davina's every waking thought in the days that followed. What, she asked herself over and over again, was his real motive for making love to her. If his name had been anything but Leo Seymour she would have gloried in the way he made her feel, but since he was who he was she couldn't rid herself of niggling suspicions. There was, of course, always the possibility that to Leo she really was exactly as he said, a woman he found attractive, and very physically attractive at that, if his behaviour the previous Sunday was anything to go by. But, argued a persistent small voice, was part of this very same attraction the fact that she was Sean Lennox's sister? By doing his utmost to make her fall in love with him, would Leo be exacting some form of revenge for that long-ago débâcle, however indirect? And once he was sure of her, what guarantee did she have that Leo wouldn't walk out of her life again without a backward glance? In one way, Davina acknowledged, it was too late to worry about it. She *had* fallen in love with Leo. His lovemaking had been enough to confirm that beyond question. Always supposing, of course, that she had ever fallen *out* of love with him in the first place, which was open to doubt.

The problem now was where she should go from here. In one way it was simple. What she wanted, had wanted subconsciously since she was seventeen years old, was to spend every waking hour with Leo—and, if she were honest, every sleeping hour too. She wanted him as her lover, however temporary the arrangement. Davina faced the fact with unblinkered eyes, knowing only too well that along that particular path lay heartbreak far worse than before. And this time recovery would be infinitely more difficult, even impossible.

She saw very little of Leo, whose time and energies were absorbed in completion of his film, and when she did see him it was only for a brief chat about his day over coffee late at night, their only physical contact a swift kiss before he left her.

Leo was blunt about his reasons a few nights later. 'I lost my head last Sunday, Davy. I never intended to let things go so far.'

Worn to shreds by sleepless nights and her first real encounter with physical frustration, Davina was equally blunt.

'As far as I'm concerned you didn't go far enough.'

Leo's eyes dilated in shock. 'Don't say things like that, Davy, unless you mean them.'

She eyed him challengingly. 'I rarely say things I don't mean.'

He loosened his collar, his colour high, to her intense gratification. 'Then perhaps you'd care to consider a suggestion I intended making once the film was finished.'

'Suggestion? An improper one, perhaps?'

Leo shrugged, his eyes holding hers with a gleam that made her wriggle in her chair. 'With any other woman I don't think for a minute it would be—improper, as you put it, but with you I don't know any more. Lately my energies are concentrated on quelling my insane desire to make love to you all the time, rather than trying to read your mind.'

Davina's eyes widened and darkened, the overt response in them bringing Leo off his chair to kneel in front of her, his hands on the arms of her chair either side of her.

'I was going to wait until you'd had time to get used to the idea of—of you and me as a pair. But since you've precipitated the whole thing, how do you feel about asking for some time off to run away with me for a holiday in some remote spot where no one's ever heard of Byron, or John Wynne Jones, or even British Telecom?' Leo picked up her hand and kissed it, his eyes meeting hers. 'Will you?'

Davina regarded him in silence. Well, here it was. Just what she had wanted. Leo, right on cue, asking her to do exactly what she wanted so badly to do. So why wasn't she throwing herself into his arms in gratitude? What was keeping her tongue-tied?

Leo waited, his body tense as a coiled spring. 'What is it, Davina?' he asked huskily. 'Are the proprieties bothering you?'

They were the last thing on her mind, at this moment. How could she put into words her fear that it wasn't taking off with him to some romantic spot that troubled her? It was the thought of coming back here to life without him afterwards that slowed down her instinctive urge to say yes.

Leo took a deep breath. 'There is an alternative, of course,' he said carefully. 'We could get married. If you like.'

Davina eyed him, dumbfounded. If *she* liked? Weren't both parties supposed to like the idea? She turned her head away. 'I don't think that's on for you and me, Leo, do you? Think how awkward family gatherings would be, just for starters.'

Leo's eyes hardened. 'I was proposing marriage to you, not your family.'

'As a proposal it lacked the necessary conviction

somehow.'

'Did it?' Leo shrugged. 'Then forget it, Davy.'

Davina suddenly lost her temper and jumped to her feet. 'OK. Let's both forget it. Only next time you ask someone the same question take my advice, phrase it with more enthusiasm. Your approach was the tiniest bit casual for most women's taste.'

'Davy——' Leo took her by the shoulders, but she shrugged his hands away.

'Time you went, I think, Leo.'

'I don't want to leave you like this.' He moved close behind her, so close she could feel the warmth of his breath on the back of her neck.

'Like what?' She turned to face him, her chin up. 'I'm fine. Now I really must get some sleep. Heavy day tomorrow.'

Leo stared down at her in defeat. 'Shall I see you tomorrow night when I come home?'

'Why not?' Her smile was bright as she bade him goodnight, and for a moment Leo hesitated, then he touched her cheek with a gentle hand and left without a farewell kiss for the first time in almost a week.

In misery Davina stood staring at the connecting door after he had gone, wondering where it all gone wrong, whether his proposal had been an impulse he had regretted the moment the words were out of his mouth.

She undressed listlessly, lecturing herself for being so idiotic about the whole thing. What exactly had she expected? Declarations of undying love? Leo had probably made those to Madeleine, and look where that had led! Nevertheless, despite all her previous conclusions, a mere holiday with him just wasn't possible. She sat on the edge of her bed, deeply depressed, then started up in alarm as the door burst open and Leo came in like a whirlwind.

'Davy, I couldn't leave it like that. What the hell happened? Where did I go wrong?' He yanked her up into his arms and raised her tear-stained face to his.

'You shouldn't be here,' she said, eyeing his thigh-length bathrobe.

'Very probably. But I couldn't stay up there in my room with those great eyes of yours haunting me. I kept thinking of what you said the other night, about not getting hurt again, and I knew for a certainty that's exactly what I'd done a second time.' Leo drew her down to sit on the edge of the bed beside him. 'Davy— listen. I want you. Meeting you again has been a revelation to me. I never dreamed I'd feel like this again about any woman, but on the other hand I can't offer you that first untarnished rapture which should be yours by right. I'm trying to be straight with you. I want you to share my life, God knows. I want it badly. But I'm years older than you. Madeleine apart, I've known far too many women, whereas you ought to be thinking of marriage with some young, enthusiastic chap with less mileage to his credit.'

'I'm not buying a second-hand car!' Davina managed a watery smile. 'And at this particular moment in time I don't want to marry *anyone* very much—not even you.'

Leo pulled her close, his cheek on her hair. 'Then what is it you want, Davy?'

She leaned her head against his shoulder, thinking hard. It was easier in some ways to think of things she didn't want, rather than those she did. One thing was crystal-clear. She didn't want Leo to go away and leave her alone. But neither did she want him with a mind even faintly preoccupied with thoughts of revenge, or regrets for a lost love. 'Couldn't we just stay the way we are, Leo?'

'Friends, you mean?' Leo's voice was almost inaudible.

'No. I thought perhaps we could be more than that.'

'Lovers?'

'Yes. Please.'

He was quiet for a long time, and Davina waited quietly, relieved the word had finally been said.

'Davy,' he said huskily at last, 'have you really thought this through?'

'Yes, I have. We share the same house as it is. It's not such a big step to sharing the same bed.'

He turned her in his arms so that he could look down into her face. 'If you were almost anyone else in the world I wouldn't hesitate. But you're Davina Lennox, daughter of a lady I like and respect very much, and, even more to the point, sister of three brothers who are all likely to object violently to any union with me unless it's legal. Just imagine Sean's reaction! He'd be certain to look on it as retaliation on my part. No one in your family would believe I sincerely *care* for you. They'd think I was just out for revenge.'

'Isn't what I think the most important thing, Leo?' Davina's eyes challenged him. 'It's me you'd be living with, not my family. I'm a grown woman now, with my own life to lead.' She shrugged. 'But if the idea doesn't appeal to you, please don't worry! As I said, I'm not seventeen any more; I don't take things to heart so much now. I promise you I won't go into a decline because you don't feel up to taking on a Lennox as a partner.'

Leo shook her, his face suddenly dark with anger. 'That's not the stumbling-block, you little idiot.' Abruptly he released her and stood up, glowering down at her. 'All right, Davina, let's get it straight.' His emphasis on her full name sounded ominously deliberate. 'I would like nothing better at this very moment than to throw you on your bed and demonstrate once and for all just how much I want us to be lovers. Do you think I'm made of stone, for God's sake? I've been living in the same house with you for weeks now; night after night of knowing you were down here, a mere few yards away, but at the same time completely out of reach.'

'Just because I'm Sean's sister,' she said bitterly. 'Not to mention Madeleine's sister-in-law!'

'I'd be lying if I said that wasn't part of it.' He thrust a hand through his hair moodily. 'But it's not only that. I genuinely don't think you're the sort of girl to enter into a relationship as casually as you're suggesting.'

'Oh, don't you?' Her eyes flashed with sudden anger. 'And just why are you so firmly convinced you're the first man I've wanted to set up house with?'

His face drained of all expression, and he stepped back. 'Of course—how stupid of me. I don't know why—I just somehow assumed——'

'That I'd been carrying a torch for you all these years?'

'Of course not!' he snapped. 'I meant that in some indefinable way you seem untouched——'

'By human hand?' She eyed him scornfully. 'Your present preoccupation with the nineteenth century must be distorting your perception, Leo. I'm contemporary. Women occupy a different place in life these days, and I'm no exception.'

There was a tense silence while they glared at each other, then with a muffled curse Leo grabbed her and began to kiss her with an air of angry purpose that frightened her considerably. She struggled and broke free, taking flight into the small hall, but Leo caught her easily, hauling her up against him.

'Right then, sweetheart; if that's the way you prefer it. Let's go back to the scene of our interrupted crime.'

He picked her up and took her into the parlour, then almost dropped her as a knock sounded on the front door. Davina stared at Leo in consternation, as he set her on her feet.

'I'll see who it is.' He eyed her suspiciously. 'Do you often get company at this time of night?'

'Only yours!' She pushed him aside. 'I'll go—it's my door.'

The knocking sounded again, louder and more urgent this time, and a male voice called her name.

'Miss Lennox. Are you there?'

'Go away,' hissed Davina to Leo, but he stood his ground in the middle of the room, shaking his head obstinately.

'Not on your life, Davy.'

Smoothing back her hair Davina tightened the girdle of her dressing-gown and unbolted the door. She opened it a crack, all her blood draining away from her face as she saw PC White, the local constable, outside on the doorstep.

'What—what is it?' she asked huskily, too terrified even to greet the man politely.

'Could I come in, Miss Lennox?' he asked, and Davina had no choice but to open the door and let him into the parlour, where the policeman greeted Leo with relief rather than speculation, Davina noted dimly. 'Good evening, sir.'

'Good evening, Constable,' answered Leo, and put an arm round Davina, who was shaking from head to foot. 'Something wrong?'

'The telephones aren't working in this part of the village—some fault on the line. A message has been passed on to me reporting an accident to Mrs Lennox. She's in hosiptal in Guildford, and Mr Joe Lennox asked his sister to get there as quickly as possible.'

'Which Mrs Lennox?' asked Leo, as Davina went paler.

The policeman consulted his notebook. 'A Mrs Margaret Lennox. She was driving home through a thunderstorm and her car went out of control on a flooded road. That's all the details I have, sir.'

Davina found her voice with an effort. 'Do you know how badly she was hurt?'

PC White's face was sympathetic. 'I'm afraid not. Mr Lennox was in a hurry to get off the phone, I think.' He looked at the briefly clad pair in some embarrassment. 'Sorry for disturbing you—with such unwelcome news, I mean.'

'Not at all,' said Leo pleasantly. 'Perhaps I should introduce myself.' He held out his hand. 'Leo Seymour, Miss Lennox's fiancé.'

The man shook his hand gravely. 'Saw you at the fête, sir. Glad to know you. If there's anything I can do——'

Davina was only half listening. Part of her threatened to panic, but the trained nurse sternly quelled it, thinking rapidly. 'If my phone is out I shan't be able to contact the practice manager, Mrs Hammond. I'd be grateful if you'd get a message to her, Constable, and explain why I won't be at work tomorrow. Tell her I'll be in touch as soon as possible.'

The policeman was patently relieved to be of some help, and went off after further assurances of his goodwill.

Davina turned to Leo. 'You'll drive me?' she asked, brusque in her anxiety.

'Of course. Give me a few minutes to dress, and we're away.'

The journey from Gloucestershire to Surrey was made in rapid time, in spite of the sheeting rain.

'Want to talk?' asked Leo, and Davina found she did. It was a kind of relief to put her fears into words. Her father had been a larger-than-life personality whose death had left a great void in his family's life. But the thought of losing her mother was different again, something Davina had never even contemplated.

'Silly, isn't it, to think of someone as immortal?' she said. 'My father was fifteen years older than my mother, which is why I've always taken it for granted she'd be around for at least that long after he died, if not longer.'

'It may be nothing serious,' said Leo soothingly, but Davina shook her head in despair.

'Joe's the sobersides of the family. He'd never have sent for me if—if——' She forced back the tears. 'Lord, Leo, you must be fed up to the teeth with me and my crises. The name Lennox spells trouble as far as you're concerned.'

'Rot,' he said briefly. 'I'm just glad I was there when you needed me.'

Davina frowned, suddenly struck by the thought that Leo might be inconveniencing himself a great deal by just taking off with her in the middle of filming, and said so anxiously. He brushed it aside casually, saying he would ring Paul Delaney as soon as they reached the hospital and knew the situation. It was past three in the morning when they were greeted at the hospital by a tired, drawn Joe Lennox, who looked taken aback when he saw Davina's companion.

'Leo? Good God! How——'

'Never mind that now!' said Davina sharply. 'How's Mother?'

Mrs Lennox, it appeared, was suffering from mild concussion, a broken wrist, severe bruising of the ribs and a sprained ankle, but otherwise wasn't as badly hurt as first suspected. Davina went chalk-white, her eyes blazing as she turned on her brother like a tigress.

'You mean to say you let me travel all the way here in the middle of the night, terrified that Mother was at death's door, when all the time—God! You swine, Joe Lennox!'

Her brother raised a hand. 'Hey, steady on, Davy. I couldn't get hold of you on the phone, and when I finally managed to raise the police in your village the line was so bad conversation was pretty difficult.'

She glared at him, murder in her eyes. 'Just you try opening the door to the police in the small hours to hear your mother's been in a car-crash, you—you insensitive blockhead! And why say I had to get there at once? Surely you knew I'd think the worst?'

Joe had obviously had enough. 'Now just you calm down, Davy. It's been a rough night for me, too, you know. And just for the record, it wasn't *I* who asked you to come, it was Mother.'

Leo put a hand on Davina's arm. The waiting-room was empty, fortunately, not that it would have mattered to Davina if it had been packed with onlookers. She shook off Leo's hand impatiently, demanding to know what her brother meant, and calmed down somewhat when she learned that Mrs Lennox, when she regained consciousness, had demanded to know how soon she could go home. When told she would be obliged to stay where she was for a while unless there was someone at home who could look after her, Mrs Lennox had informed Sister that a fully trained nurse was available, and ordered her son to send for Davina.

'Then Mother went to sleep, so I sent Sarah home to the children, and stayed on here to wait for you,' concluded Joe.

'I suppose it never even occurred to you how I was

going to get here!' said Davina tartly. 'I don't possess a car, remember.'

'It doesn't matter now,' said Leo briskly. 'I happened to be on hand, so the question's academic.'

Joe looked uncomfortable. 'I gather you live near Davy these days, Leo. Thanks a lot for giving her a lift. Very good of you. I was so taken with Mother's accident I never gave a thought to how Davy would get here.'

'Have you been in touch with Ben and Sean?' asked Davina.

'Mother said to leave that until tomorrow—today, rather.'

Davina was allowed to take a look at her mother, whose appearance was a little disquieting owing to several bruises and superficial cuts on her face. Mrs Lennox was sleeping peacefully, alone for the moment in a side ward, and the Night Sister advised Davina to return in the morning, when she would be allowed a brief visit.

'Yes, Sister, thank you, Sister,' said Davina automatically, and Sister Casualty smiled, a twinkle in her eye.

'You must be the nurse Mrs Lennox said would be arriving to take care of her.'

'*But,* Mother,' Davina said crisply to Mrs Lennox a few hours later, 'it means coming back with me to do your recuperating at Ivy Cottage.'

'Yes, dear,' said Mrs Lennox, with a meekness which confirmed she was still not herself. 'How's my car?'

'Not too bad. You—and it—were very lucky. You skidded into a ditch, but didn't tangle with another vehicle, so the car will be out of the garage in a couple of days as good as new.' And Davina proceeded to tell the tale of her midnight ride with Leo to her mother's bedside.

'So Leo drove Joe and me back to a large breakfast with Sarah, then Leo insisted on driving back to Hadfield Chase to get on with filming *Dangerous to Know.*'

'Is that the title of the film?' asked Mrs Lennox with interest. 'He must think it applies to you, too. Crisis seems to follow in your wake when Leo's around.'

Davina regarded her battered parent severely. 'Now be fair; he's only been involved over Casey and you because he decided to take up residence in Ivy Cottage—which *isn't* my fault.'

'Very true. I wonder why he chose to do it.' Mrs Lennox closed her eyes wearily. 'Sorry, darling, but I seem to need a nap again—so tiresome feeling feeble like this.'

Davina's heart smote her as she carefully chose an uninjured portion of her mother's cheek to kiss, and assured her she would feel much better very quickly. To her relief she was proved right, and a few days later Mrs Lennox was installed in Davina's room in Ivy Cottage, while Davina went back to the practice. Since Davina was able to dash home for a few minutes mid-morning, and again at lunch time, her mother was never alone for long.

'Don't fuss, Davina,' she said. 'The telephone's right alongside me, Leo's sent me enough books to last for months, and if I get fed up with reading I can be gloriously sinful and watch television in the afternoon, so run along and do your own thing, there's a good girl.'

Filming at Hadfield Chase had finished before Davina returned to Ivy Cottage with her mother, and Leo had already left for London, to prepare for his next film. The cottage had been full of flowers the day they arrived, with a letter and a parcel for Davina, telling her to sleep upstairs if she wished.

'The rent on the flat is paid up until the end of the year,' he wrote, 'so please feel free to use it as much as you like. I intend coming down myself as soon as I succeed in getting the necessary backing for the new film. One way and another I feel we have a lot of unfinished business, Davy, not least the fact that everyone in your neighbourhood is no doubt privy to the little secret I confided to PC White that night. Enclosed is the customary badge of office. Please wear it. Yours, Leo.'

The 'enclosed' was a ring; very beautiful and obviously old, a half-hoop of rubies and diamonds in a heavy claw-and-crown setting. Mrs Lennox, comfortably settled on the sofa with her foot up and her injured arm supported by a cushion, was diverted from her pleasure in Leo's lavish floral welcome by the strangled sound made by her child as Davina took out the ring.

'Something you're keeping from me?' inquired Mrs Lennox affably, and Davina explained about the arrival of the village constable late at night, when she and Leo were dressed in which could only be described as a very informal manner.

'And how exactly did Leo explain?' Mrs Lennox's eyes were bright with curiosity.

'I hardly noticed at the time, in all the anguish of the moment, but I think he just introduced himself as my fiancé,' Davina stared at the ring, frowning. 'I thought I must have imagined it, because he's never said a word since'.

'Perhaps he thought this the best way to avoid argument.' Mrs Lennox examined the ring with respect. 'Exquisite. I should wear it. Everyone at the practice will be agog, so you might as well give them something concrete by way of evidence.'

'Mother, it was a spur-of-the-moment bid to preserve my respectability, that's all. Very chivalrous, but quite unnecessary. It's not against the law to—to——'

'Spend the night with a man.'

'Precisely.'

'Except that Leo's something of a celebrity.'

'And I'm the simple village maiden, I suppose; i.e. it's OK for him, but not for me.' Davina scowled. 'Besides, I don't suppose it fits.' She slid the ring on her finger and smiled sheepishly. It fitted perfectly, and looked so beautiful that she was seized by a sudden urge to wear it permanently, and for the right reasons, rather than those given by Leo in his letter.

When Leo rang that night Davina thanked him stiffly for his kind thought, assuring him the gesture had been unnecessary. Her response to his questions was all the less spontaneous because her mother, immobilised on the sofa within earshot, was an unwilling listener-in.

'I assume you're not alone,' said Leo, amused.

'That's right.'

'Did you like the ring, Davy? Regardless of whether it's necessary or not?'

'Very much.'

'I found it in an antique shop and somehow it seemed perfect for you. Oddly enough I was sure it would fit. Did it?'

'Yes. I'll take great care of it.' Davina glanced over her shoulder towards the parlour, where her mother had put the sound up on the television in an attempt to isolate herself from the telephone conversation.

'Davy, I hope you'll take advantage of my bed while your mother's with you. It would be silly not to, particularly since I'm not in it,' added Leo with a chuckle.

'Thanks, I will,' she said breathlessly.

'Davy—don't ring off. Here's my number, in case you need me.'

Davina scribbled it obediently on the kitchen memo-pad. 'Thanks, Leo. But I'll try not to trouble you again for a bit, if I possibly can. You must be fed up with me and my traumas.'

'Don't be silly. Jack sends his love, by the way.' Leo's voice dropped a little. 'What would you say if I sent you mine, Davy?'

Since she was incapable of any reply at all Davina rang off. Mrs Lennox, with great nobility of spirit, refrained from asking any questions, obviously considering some of them superfluous, since her daughter's eyes rivalled the new ring with their glitter. However, when Davina said, elaborately casual, that she might as well take Leo up on his offer of a bed in his absence, it was plain Mrs Lennox had to exert considerable control to avoid making any comment.

'It's all right, Mother,' said Davina tartly. 'I intend occupying it solely in his absence, I assure you. And in answer to the question trembling on your lips—no, I never *have* slept in it with Leo. *Nor* down here in the chaste little cot now turned over to you, or anywhere else, for that matter,' she added. 'When I share a bed with a man I prefer just two of us snuggled up together. With Leo I'd probably have to move over to make room for the memory of Madeleine, as well.'

CHAPTER EIGHT

LIFE was very full for Davina for the next week or two. her job absorbed her by day and the evenings were taken up in watching that her impatient parent refrained from overtaxing herself. Margaret Lennox, normally a very healthy woman, had little patience with the limitations of a sprained ankle and broken wrist once her concussion was a thing of the past. Even before leaving Surrey she had considered herself well on the way to recovery, with the result that each evening Davina would return to Ivy Cottage to find her mother had somehow achieved an evening meal, and, furthermore, was none the worse for the effort.

'I do wish you'd remember that you had a nasty accident,' scolded Davina, even while enjoying her supper. 'And don't imagine you can drive that car for ages yet.'

'How can I? You take it off to the practice all the time to make sure I don't.'

'Otherwise I wouldn't have the time to pop home to check on what you're up to!'

The nights in Leo's bed were strange. To her dismay Davina found she missed him quite badly most of the time, but alone in his big, airy bedroom at night she missed him quite violently and found it hard to sleep, despite the fact that his bed was infinitely more comfortable than her own downstairs. On the third night, just before midnight, the telephone rang beside Leo's bed, startling her. Davina stared at it, then picked it up gingerly and said, 'Hello?'

111

'It's only me.' Leo's teasing voice was so much what she wanted to hear that Davina couldn't answer for a moment.

'I thought you were an obscene phone-call,' she said at last.

'If I think of you lying in my bed I'm sure I can manage to breathe heavily enough!'

'How do you know I'm in your bed?'

'You are, aren't you?'

'Yes.'

'I wish I were with you.'

Davina flushed, all on her own in the dark. 'Just because we're presumed to be engaged doesn't mean you can say things like that to me, Mr Seymour,' she said primly.

'It's God's truth, Davy. I miss you.'

It was on the tip of her tongue to say she missed him, too, but she caught herself in time. 'How's the finance campaign going?' she asked instead.

'Remarkably well. Paul Delaney's managed to get it all in train. Happily it's a fairly low-budget affair this time. Most of it will be shot in a court-room, with a few flash-backs we'll film on location in Wales.'

'Is Jack in it this time?'

'Yes, but he's a baddy. Nice change for him. A character-part really, quite a contrast to Byron.'

Leo went on chatting for some time before he finally said goodnight, sent his love to Mrs Lennox, told Davina to take care of herself, then hung up, leaving her restless for most of the night.

Davina found it hard to mention Leo's call to her mother next morning, and drove the short distance to the medical centre frowning abstractedly, her mind so taken up with Leo she almost walked past Helen Bates after parking the car.

'No need to ask what's on your mind!' Helen roared with laughter at Davina's guilty face as they went into the building together.

After that Leo took to ringing up most nights, always very late, some time after Davina was in bed. He told her how he had spent his day, the latest progress on the film and its cast, about the book from which the screenplay was taken, and sent it to her so that she could read it and let him know what she thought of it. He took pains to include her in his life and his activities, sometimes even the snags and worries, and Davina was pleased.

'Shall I come down and see you this weekend?' he asked one night, and Davina smiled radiantly into the darkness.

'Yes, if you like.' Her voice was carefully casual. 'Mother and I are still a bit limited in our activities, I'm afraid. Mother would be thrilled to see you, I know.'

'I'm glad. I'd be even more so if I thought *you* were.' Leo's voice dropped a tone. 'Are you, Davy? I don't ask for "thrilled", but I'd like to think you were—pleased.'

'I am.' It seemed pointless to deny it. '*Very* pleased,' she added for good measure, and was rewarded by a sharp intake of breath on the other end of the line.

As the weekend approached Davina was filled with a mounting excitement which acted like adrenalin, and she worked with limitless energy and enthusiasm. Nothing was too much trouble. During the extra time she put in at 'the front of the shop' as Mrs Hammond, the practice manager, liked to put it, her smile was as restorative to all the patients as the prescriptions she handed out, and her colleagues smiled knowingly and teased her, though with kindness and indulgence, since her happiness was so beautiful to behold.

It plainly worried Mrs Lennox, who was uneasy in the presence of it. 'I remember you like this once before,' she said with meaning, as Davina sang over the washing up. 'It was over the same man, too. Reluctant though I am to dampen your spirits, I can't help thinking of what happened last time.'

'This time, Mother dearest, it's different.'

'Let's hope so. When's he coming?'

'In time for lunch on Saturday.'

During Friday evening Davina washed her hair, gave herself a facepack, painted her nails and fussed with herself until Mrs Lennox begged her to stop.

'Enough's enough, Davina. This is the last episode of this serial tonight, and your blatant euphoria is ruining my concentration.'

Davina meekly sat quiet, staring at the television screen until Mrs Lennox decided it was time for bed, then helped her undress as usual and settled her comfortably. She read for a while alone in the parlour until she was satisfied her mother was sleeping, then turned out the lights and went through the communicating door to climb the stairs to Leo's bed. As she reached the top her heart lurched and she leaned limply in the doorway. The bedside lamp was on and in the bed, propped up against the headboard, was Leo, his eyes dancing in his poker-straight face.

'I couldn't wait until tomorrow,' he said, and held out his arms.

Davina just stared at him for a moment, stunned by the warmth of her reaction to the sight of him, then she ran to him, throwing herself into his waiting arms with such unguarded joy on her face that his eyes blazed in response in the split second before his head came down to hers. They melted together wordlessly, hard angles and yielding curves coming together fiercely as hands and lips found each other, wild in their discovery as he drew her beneath the covers into a dark, private world where she murmured, inarticulate in her joy as he traced every line of her body with fingers and lips, the delicacy of his touch at once a delight and a torment. Leo's hands were in her hair as he kissed her, then they slid down her body again and began a final assault on her senses, thrusting and demanding until she gasped for mercy. The instant he granted it both of them were consumed by a mounting fire that finally engulfed them in the fulfilment they burned for, silencing them both by the utter rapture of it as they lay spent in each other's arms, unwilling to separate and become two entities again.

It was a long, long time before either of them stirred. At last Leo said huskily, 'Aren't you going to say *anything,* my darling?'

Davina moved away a fraction, reluctantly. 'Hello, perhaps?'

Leo laughed softly and turned her so that she lay with her head tucked into the angle of his shoulder. 'I suppose so. You seemed struck dumb when you first saw me.'

'I was—surprised,' she said sedately, then giggled. 'I think you were, too. Eventually.'

He breathed in deeply. 'Bowled over.'

'Were you? Why? What did you expect?'

'I'm not sure. I had an idea you might be annoyed because I sneaked in unannounced. That you'd just turn tail and go back downstairs, perhaps. At best all I hoped for was a chat and a goodnight kiss.'

'Oh, dear.' Davina bit her lip and drew away a little to look up at him. 'So one way and another my welcome was a bit over the top, then!'

'No!' Leo held her closer. 'What happened was sheer magic, Davy. The expression on your face alone was something I'd never dared hope for.'

'You mean because I looked pleased to see you?'

Leo laughed unsteadily, and put a finger under her chin to turn her face up to his. 'Yes, sweetheart. Because you looked pleased to see me.'

'And showed it,' she said, her eyes laughing at him.

His darkened and he bent to kiss her, and she wriggled with pleasure, entwining her legs with his as she ran her hands through his hair, her lips opening to his with joyous spontaneity.

'Oh Davy, Davy,' he said, when he raised his head at last. 'Why couldn't you have been like this sooner? Think of the time we've wasted!'

Davina's eyes were thoughtful. 'It hasn't *been* wasted, Leo. I didn't feel like this before—not so intensely, at least. But I've missed you badly. And those late-night chats of yours made me restless——'

'Made *you* restless!' he said with feeling. 'I won't sully your ears by describing what they did to me.' His arms tightened their hold on her and Davina laughed softly.

'The bed was perfect for two after all.'

'Did you doubt it would be?'

Davina pulled away and sat up, propping herself on her hands, entirely unselfconscious of her nudity. 'I was afraid it would need to be big enough for three.' She looked hard into his upturned face. 'You, me and Madeleine.'

Leo's eyes never wavered. 'Laying it on the line as usual, my love. Well? What's the verdict? *Did* you think anyone came between us?'

Her eyes dropped. 'No. I couldn't think of anything at all except——'

'Except what?'

'The things you were doing; the things I was feeling——' Davina trailed into silence, unselfconscious no longer, burningly aware that his eyes were on her out-thrust breasts, shocked to find her nipples hardened in response. Her lips parted, and she ran the tip of her tongue over their sudden dryness as Leo lay there so very still, only his eyes moving as they roamed over every visible part of her, from the edge of the quilt, where it lay across her hips, up over her breasts to her hair and her flushed, wide-eyed face. He reached out a hand and drew away the covers very slowly until he could see all of her, then with a sudden impatience pulled her down to him and began to make love to her all over again.

This time Leo was less gentle, less patient, and for an instant at first Davina was conscious of faint surprise, thinking it should all have been more leisurely a second time, but suddenly he seemed to lose control of his need of her and she stopped thinking all together, gasping as he thrust her beneath him and took possession of her with such desperation she yielded herself up to him completely, giving him everything he craved. Leo was trembling when it was over, patently overwhelmed by his own urgency and her unrestrained response to it.

'I'm sorry, I'm sorry,' he muttered hoarsely into her hair, holding her cruelly tight. 'I didn't mean—I couldn't——'

'Don't!' She put a finger on his lips. 'Please don't be sorry.'

A shudder ran through Leo's body. 'I meant I was sorry for being so selfish, for hurting you perhaps, Davy. Not for anything else. You give so unstintingly. I only wish . . .'

Davina drew away to lie quietly, looking at his face, which was dewed with sweat still, his brows drawn together over his half-closed eyes as he returned her look in silence.

'What do you wish, Leo?' she whispered.

He smiled crookedly. 'That I were younger—less second-hand. That I could bring you the same wonder I could see on your face as I made love to you.'

Davina's eyes were tranquil. 'If I don't mind, Leo, why should you? I know about Madeleine—who better? And I'm not stupid enough to think there haven't been a lot of others since. I could hardly expect a man of your age to be inexperienced, anyway, could I? And I'm not sure I'd want you to be. Tonight would have been a right old fiasco if *both* of us had been amateurs.'

Leo's face softened and he moved closer to her, kissing her lips very delicately. 'I fancy you haven't made love very much before at all, have you, sweetheart?'

She looked away. 'No. Not all that much.'

'You will in future, if I have my way!' He laughed unsteadily. 'Say you'll marry me, Davina. I'd do my best to make you happy, I promise. Always.'

Davina turned over on her back, pulling the quilt up to her chin. 'We'd have to clear up a few things first.'

Leo slid out of bed and pulled on a dressing-gown before sitting at the end of the bed to look at her. 'If we're to have a serious discussion I'll think better at a distance.' He smiled at her, his eyes dancing, and Davina grinned.

'Right then, Mr Seymour. If you're really serious about this——'

'Deadly serious, Miss Lennox.' And he meant it, Davina could see. She nodded in a businesslike way.

'I would need an assurance or two before I agree to what is, for me, a very binding promise. If I do marry you, I would expect to stay married.'

Leo looked at her levelly. 'You mean that, unlike another lady who shall be nameless, you wouldn't go running off with someone else, nor would you expect me to do likewise.'

Davina inclined her head gravely. 'I would take that as read. What I'm really asking is whether you still, even in the slightest, carry a torch for Madeleine. If so, no deal. However good we are together in bed, Leo, I want it good in the other ways a marriage is good; companionship, friendship, fidelity. The kind of marriage my parents had. I'm not prepared to settle for anything less. Nor will I put up with any shadowy thirds in the relationship, even though I fully understand I'm not, for you, that first careless rapture you mentioned.'

Leo's eyes were deadly serious for once below the tawny hair flopping untidily over his forehead. 'Madeleine means no more to me now than a mistake I made in the past. It's over, Davy, and has been for a long time. I've met her now and again over the years, you know—pretty inevitable in our profession—but it's just like meeting an old acquaintance, nothing more.'

Davina regarded him searchingly for some time, then nodded briefly. 'OK, then.'

'What do you mean—OK?'

'I'll marry you.'

Leo sighed in exasperation. 'That's a bit casual, Davy.'

'What do you want me to say?'

'I don't know. Something more memorable, I suppose.'

Davina smiled at him cheerfully. 'How about "I'm deeply honoured by your proposal, Mr Seymour, and take great pleasure in accepting it"? Will that do?'

Leo got up and moved to stand by the bed, looking down at her. 'It's better, I suppose, but I feel I should point out that when you were stating your requirements for this marriage of yours you made no reference to the emotions. *Do* you care for me, Davina?'

'Yes,' she said briefly. 'Otherwise I wouldn't marry you. Now, if you'll hand me my nightshirt I'll get myself back downstairs to my sofa. Mother is a very understanding parent, but I don't think I should spend the night up here with you, just the same.'

'Good God!' Leo sounded stricken as he searched under the bed. 'Davy, I'm sorry, I haven't even asked how your mother is!' He held out the crumpled garment, looking penitent. 'You rather drove everything out of my head, one way and another.'

Davina chuckled as she pulled on the nightshirt and slid out of bed. 'Very flattering! Anyway, Mother's fine. She's off to Manchester to Hetty and Ben in a few days' time, now she's mobile. But by train, I hasten to add. I've put my foot down on the subject of driving, pro tem. Come down and see her in the morning.'

'I intend to.' Leo drew her to him, rubbing his cheek against her. 'I want to ask her a favour.'

'What's that?'

'I want her daughter. Do you thing she'll let me have her?'

Davina drew back, leaning against his linked arms, the look in her eyes kindling an answering flame in Leo's. 'I'll put in a good word,' she said huskily, then closed her eyes as he kissed her. The kiss went on and on, until both of them were shaking.

'Stay!' said Leo in a stifled voice. 'Don't leave now, for God's sake, darling.'

'I must.' She tore herself away, breathing unevenly, and ran for the door. 'See you in the morning.'

Downstairs in the parlour Davina lay on the sofa under a blanket, shivering with cold and frustration, wondering why she had been so adamant about leaving him. It was some time before the truth dawned on her.

When Leo made love to her she lost herself in him utterly. It was frightening. At this point Davina gave up trying to sleep and switched on a lamp to look at the ring on her finger, brooding over whether she was doing the right thing in marrying Leo Seymour. But he was the only man she had ever really felt deeply for, so why not? To hell with Madeleine. Even if Leo *did* have the odd lingering feeling for her, surely one Davina Lennox had enough bottle to fight it—*and* win. It was worth the risk. There was no remote possibility that she could ever experience with anyone else the feelings Leo roused in her. Davina flushed at the realisation that she wanted to experience them again, and as soon as possible. Only the strictest self-restraint stopped her from creeping upstairs and into his bed at that very minute, and with a muffled groan she rolled off the sofa and tiptoed to the kitchen to fill the kettle.

'If you're making tea, I'll have some.' Her mother limped into the kitchen, looking heavy-eyed. 'What are you doing down here, darling? Something wrong?'

'No. Leo came tonight instead of tomorrow, so I'm sleeping on the sofa.'

'Very badly, by the look of you.'

'I was a bit chilly, that's all.' Davina took a tray into the parlour and settled her mother on the sofa. 'Damn! I said I'd do Helen's Saturday morning tomorrow. I thought Leo wouldn't be here until lunch time.'

'You're a muggins when it comes to your job, Davina.' Mrs Lennox sipped her tea gratefully. 'That tastes wonderful. Thank you, darling.'

'Leo'll be down in the morning to see you, Mother, so you can tell him I'll be home about twelve. You can manage the lunch by yourself, can you? I feel guilty, leaving it all to you.'

'I've already made the casserole, which is busy at this

very moment absorbing all its wine, garlic, rosemary, *et al,* ready to amaze Leo's taste-buds tomorrow—today, rather. A few vegetables as accompaniment won't wear me out, I promise. Bring some French bread with you, and a couple of cartons of cream—oh, and that wonderful single Gloucester cheese they make at the dairy, while you're at it.'

The morning was busy, as usual, but it dragged for Davina, who was consumed with impatience to get home to Leo. Nevertheless her smile was much in evidence as she dealt with patients, answered the telephone, checked the prescriptions Mrs Hammond made up and, finally, helped the doctor with a hysterical child and trembling mother, while a cut on the child's chin was stitched. It seemed an age before the doors of the practice were finally locked and she was free to go.

'Thank goodness that's over,' said Mrs Hammond fervently. 'I say, that's rather a nice piece of machinery in our car park, Davina—the car I mean, not the young man leaning against it. Though he's rather gorgeous too—could he be waiting for you, I wonder?'

Davina's heart performed a somersault as Leo, his hair gleaming redly in the sunlight, caught sight of her and smiled. Every instinct prompted her to run to him, but she walked towards him as slowly as she could, completely forgetting an amused Mrs Hammond as Leo closed the space between them more rapidly, taking her in his arms to kiss her with unabashed enthusiasm, oblivious of several interested passers-by.

'Good morning, darling.' He grinned as he released her. 'I thought you'd changed your mind and run away, so I came to get you.'

Since Mrs Hammond was hovering Davina had no choice but to introduce her, then was obliged to do the same when Dr Mike Roberts came out to his car, and a few minutes were spent in polite exchanges before it was possible to leave.

'Come on, then,' said Leo urgently, as the others left. 'Let's go.'

'Shopping first. Mother wants a few things.'

'No she doesn't. I've already taken her shopping.'

Davina stared as they got in the car. 'You mean *you* went round the village shops?'

Leo nodded smugly as he reversed the Jaguar out of the car park. 'Your mother had a great time. Introduced me to everyone she saw. A lot of people remembered me from the fête, anyway.'

'Oh, boy! I bet she had a ball.'

'Told everyone I was your fiancé. Went down terribly well, I thought. A *succès fou,* you might say.'

'No I wouldn't, I was hopeless at French in school. I wasn't exceptionally good at anything. I'm not now,' she added candidly.

Leo took a hand off the wheel to grasp hers. 'Don't ever say that again.' His voice had lost its banter. 'You're a qualified nurse, which needs brains, guts and determination, not to mention a warm, kind personality. And you possess them all. You're a beautiful girl, Davina Lennox, not only your undeniably attractive exterior, but inside too, which is where it matters. So no putting yourself down in future. Right?'

Taken aback, Davina nodded meekly, then pointed out that Leo had taken the wrong turning. He informed her he was taking her for a little spin before lunch, with Mrs Lennox's full approval.

'So where are we going?'

'Just along here.' Leo manoeuvred the car down a bumpy farm track and parked it near a gate leading to a field full of cows who were grazing far too greedily to notice the long, claret-coloured car, even less the two humans inside, locked in each other's arms.

'Don't ever do that to me again,' muttered Leo against Davina's mouth after a long, breathless interval.

'Do what?'

'Leave me wanting you so much I was ready to gnaw at the wallpaper! Dear God, Davy—haven't you any idea what you do to me?'

Davina became very busy with some hairpins which had become inextricably tangled with her sweater. 'Some,' she admitted. 'I spent a pretty restless night myself.'

'I fancy I've found the remedy.' His eyes danced in their familiar way, quickening her pulse as usual as he took a document from the glove-compartment of the car. 'There you are. Not the cure for love, Davy, but a remedy for this terrible affliction I'm suffering from.'

Davina eyed him severely. 'Are you being coarse?'

Leo drew away, looking injured. 'I meant the pain of existing without you. If you'll unfold that document you'll find it's a special licence, which will legally allow me to have you and hold you for the rest of my life—and, my angel, entitles me to begin doing so as soon as we can arrange it.'

Davina began to laugh. 'Why go to all that expense, you idiot? We could have been married in the usual way in a few weeks.'

Leo pulled her back into his arms. 'Not soon enough. I've had a word with your mother; permission asked and granted, by the way, and she thought next Saturday would be the earliest it could be done. So next Saturday it is.'

'Hey! You're supposed to be marrying *me*, not my mother!'

Leo looked deep into her eyes, holding her face in his cupped hands. 'Not *supposed* to be, Davy. I am. So be quiet and kiss me.'

Since it was what she wanted to do most of all anyway, Davina did as he said, and it was some time before the Jaguar completed a tricky three-point turn on the grassy track, and returned to Ivy Cottage.

Lunch was festive. Leo's expeditions round the shops had yielded up some celebratory claret to drink with Mrs Lennox's admirable casserole, and the three of them were pleasantly mellow as they sat over coffee afterwards. Then Davina was struck by a sobering thought.

'I hate to put a damper on things,' she said, biting the tip of her finger. 'But isn't this wedding going to be a trifle—well—awkward?'

'Because of Madeleine and Sean, you mean?' Mrs Lennox had never been one to beat about the bush. 'Simple, Davina. Unless you're dead set on a big do I suggest you don't invite them, or the rest of the family. Easier all round.'

Davina frowned. 'But——' She met her mother's calm eyes. 'You mean don't have *any* guests at all?'

Mrs Lennox nodded. 'Leo will want a best man, of course. And perhaps you'd fancy inviting your friend Candida. But I should leave the family out of it. Remember how Ben and Joe felt when Sean ran off with Madeleine?' She turned to Leo. 'However Sean—and of course Madeleine—may have behaved, the rest of us were appalled. All our sympathies were with you. Except, of course, when you took to hounding Davina for a while.'

Davina jumped up restlessly, and went to make more coffee. 'For heaven's sake let's forget about the past.'

Leo followed her to the kitchen, taking her in his arms

while the kettle boiled. 'Don't be upset, Davy. Better to talk openly about everything, yes?' And he kissed her so tenderly that the momentary pang of misgiving subsided.

Mrs Lennox restored normality by suddenly asking if Leo imagined her motive for suggesting the small wedding was economy. 'It *does* sound rather miserly,' she said, frowning.

Leo laughed and sat down, pulling Davina on his lap. 'Personally I think it's a terrific idea. What man really wants hundreds of guests and a big church ceremony?' He sobered and looked searchingly at Davina. 'On the other hand, maybe that's what you've been dreaming of all your life, little one. *You* choose. I'll do whatever you want. You can have Sean, Madeleine and the entire population of the village on hand if you like. Whatever you want, you shall have.'

'Something quiet, with no fuss,' said Davina firmly. 'With Jack for best man, and perhaps the Delaneys will come, Leo. I'll invite Helen Bates and her husband, and Candida, of course. She's between men at the moment, so she'll jump at the chance of meeting Jack. And that should do. I'll ring round my big brothers and explain.'

'No,' said Margaret Lennox firmly. 'That's my job. After all, it was my idea. But what about the wedding breakfast? Shall I——?'

'No!' said Leo and Davina in unison, then laughed together, and Leo kissed his future bride lovingly on the nose.

'I'll see if they can do a rush job in the Bull,' said Davina. She looked at Leo uncertainly. 'What about *your* family, Leo?'

He shook his head. 'My parents are both dead.'

'That's it then.' Davina settled comfortably against Leo's shoulder. 'Am I allowed to ask the real reason for the rush to tie the knot?'

For a moment the gleam in Leo's eye persuaded her he was about to shock her mother, but he shocked his fiancée instead by stating that almost immediately afterwards he was taking her off to the wilds of Wales to shoot the flashback sequences of the new film. 'I may be away as long as six weeks, my lovely, and I've no intention of leaving you behind.'

'But Leo—my job!' Davina looked stunned.

'They can get someone else, child,' said Mrs Lennox matter-of-factly. 'Explain the circumstances, give your week's notice and go off with Leo to Wales.'

'Unless,' said Leo very quietly, 'you don't want to.'

Davina kissed him on the mouth, not in the least concerned that her mother was looking on. 'Oh, I want to,' she said. 'So I'll do as Mother says. This time.'

'Whereas after next Saturday I assume you'll do as *I* say.'

'Assume what you like, husband-to-be, it's a free country. But I shouldn't count on it!'

CHAPTER NINE

IT WAS late in the evening the following Saturday before Mr and Mrs Leo Seymour arrived at Ty Mawr, one-time local manor house in a remote corner of Mid-Wales, now converted into a hotel catering for guests who liked seclusion, scenery, and plain, exquisitely cooked food.

'Nice walks round here,' remarked the boy who helped Leo carry their luggage up to their room. 'Fishing too.' He eyed Leo's physique. 'And we've got a bit of a gym in the cellar if you fancy some weight-training.'

'Thank you.' Laughter quivered in Leo's voice. 'I'll remember that if I'm at a loose end.'

'These rooms used to be the attic,' said the boy as he threw open the door for them. 'My father had it made into this self-contained suite, nice and private, no one else on this floor.' He flushed with pleasure as Leo pressed a banknote into his hand. *'Thanks!* I hope you'll be comfortable.'

'It's lovely,' Davina assured him. And it was. A row of four dormer windows let the final after-glow of sunset into a long, low-ceilinged room where bright woven-wool bedcover and curtains contrasted with solid Welsh oak furniture. There were flowers on a low table drawn up near chintz-covered sofa and chairs in one half of the room, and a door stood ajar at the far end to give a glimpse of a luxuriously fitted bathroom.

'I should have carried you over the threshold,' said Leo. He put an arm round his new bride as she leaned at one of the windows to look at the beautiful wild landscape of mountains and river outside. 'But I think our young friend might have been embarrassed.'

Davina smiled at him. 'He'll expect you in the gym first thing in the morning, you know.'

'Then he'll be disappointed.' Leo drew her round into his embrace. 'The only place I intend to be tomorrow morning, Mrs Seymour, is in that very substantial-looking bed with my wife, for as long as she'll allow me to linger there.'

'That depends.'

'On what?'

'How tired she is.'

Leo kissed her lingeringly. 'If I have anything to do with it she'll be *very* tired indeed.'

'Ah, but I'm a lot younger than you!' said Davina wickedly, and danced away from him. 'And I'm hungry. Will they still have anything to eat, do you think?'

Leo glanced at his watch. 'In twenty minutes precisely Mrs Wynne Jones will bring us some supper——'

'*Who?*' demanded Davina incredulously.

'I kept it as a little surprise. Delyth and Owen, who welcomed us downstairs are Jack's uncle and aunt. That's how we came to know about Ty Mawr. We've taken it over while we're shooting.' Leo loked smug. 'Jack has relatives all over Wales, if you can believe him.'

Davina smiled wryly. 'So peace and quiet lasts only until Monday when the others move in.'

'Tuesday. I begged a day's grace. Jack had some very ribald comments which I shall leave entirely to your imagination, the gist of which was that I was a very lucky bloke, and he would be only too happy to be in my shoes.' Leo looked down at his elegantly shod feet.

'Nevertheless the only reason I shall take said shoes off is to go to bed with my new, very beautiful and—yes—blushing bride.'

'Can't you think of anything but bed?'

'No.'

Davina laughed and unlocked her case. 'Well, *I* can. I want a bath and a great deal of food. I was too excited to eat much lunch.'

'So I noticed.' Leo gave her a swift kiss. 'I'll go down to the bar and have a drink with Jack's uncle. Don't be long.'

Davina lay in the bath for exactly ten minutes, then towelled herself dry and sprayed herself liberally with the expensive French perfume given her by Candida as an extra to the pair of porcelain pot-pourri jars that were her official wedding gift. The scent was guaranteed to distract a man from absolutely anything he was doing, even watching his favourite sport on television, according to Candida, and as Davina sniffed rapturously she felt sure her friend was right.

Undecided whether to dress again or simply put on the exquisite peignoir and nightdress sent by Hetty, Davina eventually opted for her own purchase of honey-coloured satin pyjamas, then brushed her hair loose from the chic knot devised by the hairdresser to suit the wide-brimmed yellow hat worn for the wedding. She left her face to its own devices and filled in the remaining time by unpacking; first her own clothes, then Leo's. There was an exciting sense of intimacy in putting away his shirts and underwear, and hanging up the expensive designer jackets and trousers along with the much-worn denims and sweaters packed for work. There was even a leather jacket that reminded her of the one Leo had worn on that never-to-be-forgotten day long ago. Davina paused with it in her hands, her eyes absent as she thought of the seventeen-year-old with stars in her eyes. There were stars in her eyes tonight, too, she found as she looked in the mirror, then Leo's face appeared in the mirror alongside hers, his eyes tender as he slid her arms round her.

'And who *is* the fairest of them all?' He turned her in his embrace. 'You don't need to look in a mirror. You can take it from me, my darling, *you* are.'

What promised to be a very lengthy embrace was interrupted by a knock on the door and the arrival of their hostess herself, who had brought her young son with her to help with a trolley laden with hot baked ham served with a cream and herb sauce, tiny potatoes, green beans from the hotel kitchen garden, and for pudding a raspberry pie and a jug of thick yellow cream.

'And this comes with Jack's compliments,' said Delyth Wynne Jones, smiling as she produced a bottle of Bollinger champagne in a silver bucket.

When they were alone Leo smiled rather wryly. 'Jack manages to make his presence felt even *in absentia,* doesn't he?'

'It was a very nice thought,' said Davina firmly and toasted her bridegroom with her glass of champagne. 'To us, Leo, may we always be as happy as we are tonight.'

'Amen to that.' Leo raised his own glass in response, his eyes very intent as they gazed into hers. 'Do you know, Davy, I really never have been happier than I am right now.'

Her eyebrows rose. 'Never?'

He shook his head, his eyes very steady. 'Never.'

Davina's smile was radiant. 'Then let's repeat our toast, husband. To us. For ever and ever.'

Leo rose to his feet, motioning her to follow suit, and drank deeply from his glass. 'To us, Davina Seymour.

For ever and ever.'

Davina's spirits were effervescent as they began on the meal and talked over the day and all the fun of the wedding breakfast, not least of which had been the witty, audacious speech from their famous best man. Both of them had enjoyed their simple wedding to the full, not even put out by the photographers and reporters who had somehow got wind of it and subjected the rising young film director and his bride to a barrage of questions and popping flash-bulbs.

It was much later when Leo, his hair damp from the shower, joined his bride in the wide bed at last. 'You do realise, Mrs Seymour, that it is eight days since we first and last occupied a bed together? And that was only for an hour or so. I've been forced to survive more than a week with only a meagre kiss or two.'

Davina, taken aback to find herself suddenly shy, gave a stifled little laugh. 'You've been in London the whole time, so it was hardly possible for anything else.'

'Not that I'd have been allowed anything more had I been there, I fancy.' Leo drew her into his arms very gently. 'Nor would I have asked it, Davy. Until now. And even now I'm perfectly happy just to hold you like this until we go to sleep if that's the way you'd prefer it. Because something tells me my bride is suffering from a slight attack of bridal nerves. Am I right?'

Davina turned her head into his shoulder. 'Yes. Silly, isn't it, after——'

Leo laughed softly and cradled her against him. 'No. Endearing. Besides, last week you weren't expecting it to happen. Now you are—and you've got cold feet.'

Davina was racked with guilt, because he was so right. 'Leo, I'm such an idiot. It isn't that I don't want—don't feel——'

Leo hushed her, stroking her hair, silencing her

apologies, making her laugh at last by telling her about Lord Byron, who was reputed to have disposed of his brand-new bride's virginity on the sofa before dinner on their wedding-day. 'I hope I can be more forbearing than that, at least, my sweet. Go to sleep, relax. We've all the time in the world.'

And Davina, worn out after all the excitement of the day, eventually fell asleep in her husband's arms, warm and secure in the knowledge that she was where she most wanted to be at last. Whe she woke it was still dark. For a moment she was disorientated, then happiness washed over her as she realised the constriction about her waist was the hard, muscular arm of her new husband, who, it seemed, was bent on binding her to him even in his sleep.

Davina lay very still for a long time, savouring this new pleasure of waking up in the same bed as Leo, listening to his deep, even breathing, smiling to herself in the darkness at the sheer wonder of it. She turned her head very carefully to look at his sleeping face, at his profile, sharply etched against the faint light coming from the windows, and her heart was touched by his tenderness and the forbearance he had joked about. Not many men would have behaved with such restraint. Certainly none of those she had come across in her nursing days, nor any of her escorts since.

As if he felt her scrutiny, Leo's eyes opened, and he smiled.

'Sorry,' she whispered. 'I tried to lie still.'

'Sorry! Why should I want to sleep when I have you in my arms? Sheer waste!' He touched his lips to her hair. 'Feel better now?'

Davina not only felt better, she felt sudden excitement at his touch. 'Sorry I was such a ninny last night, Leo— straight out of the Ark!' And she turned and found his

mouth with hers, making her apology in the way she
hoped he would like best. He tensed, his arm tightening
as she touched the tip of her tongue very delicately to his
parted lips, running it over them then sliding her tongue
inside his mouth to caress his.

Leo gasped and caught her to him, rolling over so that
she lay beneath him. 'Is this where you want to be?' he
demanded fiercely.

'How explicit do I have to be? Make love to me!'

'With infinite pleasure!' He began by removing her
beautiful new satin pyjamas, and Davina helped him,
abruptly impatient, giving a little purr of contentment
as she wriggled close to him, exulting as the muscles of
his back grew taut beneath her searching hands. During
their previous time together Leo had been the initiator
in all the opening moves in the game of love, but this
time Davina found ways of her own; new, instinctive
ways that inflamed her husband to such an extent that
his control snapped and he took her with such tender
violence that she cried out in unashamed ecstasy as
shock waves of fulfilment convulsed her body, even
before his answering groan signalled the final frenzy of
release his body found in hers. They remained locked in
an embrace which renewed itself after only a short time
of quiescence, the rapture overtaking them once more
before they slept, only to wake again, to slower, less
frenetic lovemaking, the morning sun illuminating each
rapt, wondering face to the other as they scaled the
heights of physical pleasure in unison.

'You are quite extraordinary, Mrs Seymour,' said
Leo, when they were quiet at last.

Davina flopped over on her stomach, her chin
propped up on her hands as she looked down at his face.
'In what way?'

'Because you contrive to be simultaneously shy yet

blazingly sexy. It annihilates me.' His eyes were dancing in the way she had loved the first moment she set eyes on him, and something in her expression made him say quickly, 'What is it?'

'Nothing I'm going to tell you, Mr Seymour, or you'd have a swelled head.'

'Does that mean you think I'm sexy too?'

'Sexy, yes. But shy you're not. Neither am I, really.'

'*I* think you are. However many scalps you have to your credit. And there have been a fair number, I assume, unless the male population of Gloucestershire suffers from myopia.'

'Are you questioning me on my past?' she said indignantly. 'Because if so I shan't tell you a thing. I haven't asked you about *your* past.'

'You know the worst bit!' he retorted, and caught her hand. 'And don't turn away, because I flatly refuse to let my insanity over Madeleine lurk in the background like some closet-skeleton we mustn't mention. Agreed?'

'Agreed.'

'Good. From now on I promise to cleave only unto Davina Alethea Seymour, until death us do part. Though I did waver for a moment when I heard the Alethea bit!'

Davina giggled. 'Grandmother's name.'

'Ah!' Leo eyed her speculatively. 'Will you want *our* daughter named after her grandmother?'

Davina felt startled. Children? 'I—I suppose so. Do you want a family, Leo?'

'One day. But not for years yet, Davy. Let's enjoy each other's company exclusively for a while.' His eyes gleamed. 'And I do enjoy your company, little wife. Both in bed and out of it.'

So pleased she could only be flippant, Davina pulled her hand away and got out of bed. 'Well, it's only out of it pro tem, because I'm starving and I want a big, hearty breakfast, then a long, healthy walk.' She pulled on her dressing-gown and went to the nearest window. 'Come on, lazybones. It's a beautiful day.'

Leo lay with his arms folded behind his head, watching her. 'Very beautiful,' he agreed. 'And it would still be beautiful even if it were pouring with rain. A risk Jack said we'd run if we chose to stay at Ty Mawr, by the way.'

'Nonsense! The sun's shining, the birds are singing— and my stomach's rumbling, so do come *on*, Leo.'

They spent an idyllic period together, utterly content in each other's company. They went walking in the valley, climbed some of the gentler mountain slopes, drove round the countryside to recommended beauty-spots, then returned to Ty Mawr to enjoy Delyth Wynne Jones's matchless cooking, every last shadow between them banished in their new-found intimacy.

'A pity your period of peace will be so short-lived,' said Owen Wynne Jones before dinner the second evening. 'Once Jack arrives on the scene there'll be pandemonium as usual.'

'Very true,' sighed Leo, 'but I've got a schedule to keep to, unfortunately.' He toasted Davina silently with his glass. 'Otherwise I would have postponed filming for a week or so.'

'Or we could have been married later on when it was finished,' she pointed out.

'I wasn't prepared to wait,' said Leo bluntly, and watched with enjoyment as colour rose in his bride's face.

'You shouldn't say things like that in public,' she scolded later when they were in their room.

'I was merely stating the incontrovertible truth, Davy. I might warn you I'm not prepared to wait now, either, so for God's sake come here and kiss me.'

Owen Wynne Jones had not been exaggerating. Jack brought uproar in his wake, since a fair number of the film crew arrived with him to take up residence at Ty Mawr, including the producer, Paul Delaney, who was the bearer of bad tidings. Briony Carter, given an important part in the new film, as promised by Leo, had been taken ill.

'Glandular fever?' said Leo incredulously. 'At her age?'

Davina assured him it was perfectly possible, since Briony was little older than herself, and for the time being highly infectious, quite apart from how wretched she must be feeling. Someone else would need to step in fairly quickly if their time in Wales wasn't to be a complete disaster.

'Joanna?' said Leo without much hope, but Paul shook his head gloomily. 'She's due in LA shortly to do a television series, remember?'

'God, yes.' Leo thrust his hands through his hair, looking distraught, while Jack hastily procured drinks for everyone from his uncle, in an effort to help. 'Briony was exactly right for the girl in this—that rather delicate, fragile look. Perfect for the rape scene here, and the trial later on. Damn, damn, damn.'

Davina melted away, deciding her presence was extraneous until the problem was sorted out, and found Gareth Wynne Jones returning home from school on his bicycle as she wandered through the gardens of the hotel.

'Have the film people come yet, Mrs Seymour?' he asked eagerly, jumping off.

Davina smiled at him warmly, not only because he was an engaging boy, but because it was so wonderful to hear herself addressed as 'Mrs Seymour'. 'Yes, Gareth, the gang's all here. The vehicles are parked in the paddock.'

'Dad says they're going to use the old part of the house to film some of the scenes,' he said blissfully. 'D'you think I'll be able to watch?'

'Of course. Why? Do you fancy an actor's life?'

'*Duw,* no! I want to be a cameraman!'

Davina laughed and promised to ask Leo's permission for Gareth to sit in sometimes, then went with him to the kitchen where his mother, with the aid of extra helpers from the village, was deep in preparations to feed the influx of guests. Davina demanded something to do, and her practical hostess took her at her word, giving her the task of laying the tables for dinner, but after that refused further help.

'Not on your honeymoon, dear,' said Delyth Wynne Jones, smiling. 'Go back to that gorgeous husband of yours and tell him you deserve a drink.'

Davina's gorgeous husband was looking distinctly put out when she went back to the bar. He was arguing with Paul Delaney, and backed up by Jack Wynne Jones, whose handsome face was black with disapproval as he joined in the violent discussion.

The rest of the men in the bar greeted Davina with enthusiasm, and insisted on buying her a drink, teasing and apologetic for their intrusion on her honeymoon. She laughed with them, comfortable in their company, but cast a worried glance now and then at the trio of men arguing in undertones on the far side of the room. At last Leo detached himself from the other two and came to take Davina by the hand.

'Come on, Davy. Nearly time for dinner. Let's leave this lot to their beer.'

She looked at him searchingly as they went upstairs to

their room. 'What's up, Leo? Problems over Briony's replacement?'

'Yes,' he said flatly, and closed the door behind them, taking her into his arms. He buried his face in her hair. 'Lou Winters, the backer, wants Madeleine for Briony's role.'

Davina stiffened. 'Why?' she asked, when she could speak calmly.

'Lou put up the money for the play she's in at the moment. Thinks she's the greatest. Second Vivien Leigh, according to him.' Leo kept his cheek against her hair. 'If I want to keep his money we cast Madeleine as the girl.'

Davina let out her breath in a sudden whoosh. 'You don't think she's right for the part?'

Leo took her by the shoulders, staring down at her. 'She's probably better for it than Briony, and a hell of a sight better known; more of a draw.'

'And she *does* look a bit like Vivien Leigh.'

'That's not the point——'

'You mean you don't think you can bear to have her around?' Davina looked at him steadily, and Leo shrugged, frowning.

'*I* couldn't care less. It's you I'm thinking of. How do you think I feel about subjecting you to Madeleine's presence on our honeymoon, for God's sake?'

'I know it's awkward. But if it means the difference between doing the film and not doing it I don't see you have much choice.' She smiled at him crookedly. 'As long as you don't want her to share our room.'

Blood rushed to Leo's face and he grabbed her to him, kissing her roughly. 'I don't want her here at all. *This* is what I want, and this—and this——'

'Now?' she protested faintly. 'We'll be late for dinner.'

'Do you care?' he muttered, picking her up.

'Not a lot——' Davina gasped as he bent his head to her breast. 'Oh, please——'

'Please what?' Leo sat down with her on the bed, holding back her head by her hair as he moved his parted lips down her exposed throat until they reached her breast again. 'Shall I do this? Shall I stop?' He thrust her flat, his eyes locked with hers until the final moment when his body blotted out the world and Davina's eyes shut tightly, her teeth drawing blood from her bottom lip as he took her on the swift, accelerating journey towards the culmination they sought with new desperation, as though their very survival depended on the glorious climax they achieved in unison.

A long time afterwards Leo drew away to look down into her face, breathing unevenly. 'Only you, Davy. Now and always. Madeleine was the past. You are the present and the future—and you're all mine. But remember, always, that jealousy is my greatest failing. I admit it, so never give me cause for it, Davy. Othello is someone I can relate to only too easily.' His voice was jerky, staccato, as though the words were forced out of him, as his eyes blazed down into hers. Davina stared back, mesmerised, totally overcome by their wild lovemaking and the harsh sincerity of Leo's voice.

'Would you smother me then, if I made you jealous?' she asked, trying for lightness.

He breathed in deeply. 'I hope you'll never put me to the test.' And he bent his head and kissed her with such emphasis she was dazed when he finally set her on her feet. 'Come on, my sleepy darling. Let's shower and get dressed.'

Since Leo insisted they shower together the process took far longer than it should have, and by the time they reached the dining-room everyone else was half-way through dinner. Leo ignored Jack's pointed comments on their tardiness, and apologised to Mrs Wynne Jones as she brought in their soup. She brushed it aside.

'No trouble, Mr Seymour. Your wife was a great help beforehand, and in any case it's easier not having everyone to see to at the same time.'

Leo had deliberately seated Davina so that her back was to the room, and she was grateful, deeply conscious that every man there knew perfectly well why they were late.

'Tomorrow night I'll make sure we're dead on time,' she muttered darkly as they ate.

'Then we'll need to go upstairs to change a lot earlier.' Leo grinned at her, unperturbed, and Davina relaxed.

'You'd better tell Paul to get in touch with Madeleine's agent,' she reminded him.

Leo scowled. 'I suppose so. God, what a situation! Do you suppose Sean's likely to join the happy band too?'

Davina shook her head. 'I think he's still in South America.'

Despite her doggedly sensible attitude Davina was not looking forward to having Madeleine at Ty Mawr, and her nerves were stretched taut as violin strings the night before her sister-in-law was due to arrive. Leo knew quite well how she felt and did everything in his power to reassure her, nevertheless he was quite obviously astonished when Davina told him in bed, late that night, that she quite liked Madeleine really.

'If Sean had brought her home as Joe and Ben did with their wives my feelings towards her would have been just the same as towards Hetty and Sarah. But Madeleine happened to be your property, which was the first thing against her because I was so violently in love with you.'

'*Were* you, Davy?' Leo said softly.

'Yes. But I grew out of it. As I was saying—ow! That hurt!' She removed her shoulder out of range of his teeth, which had nipped her bare skin.

'Admit you're *still* in love with me,' he ordered.

Davina had no intention of committing herself. 'I'm very fond of you. But, as you once said to me, one can't expect to experience that first fine careless rapture twice.'

Leo heaved over on his back and lay staring at the ceiling. 'Did I say that?'

'Yes. To continue: I like Madeleine, as I said, now all the dust has settled. But I think Sean should stay home more, or write a book or something. She misses him.' Davina eyed his profile frostily. 'Are you listening?'

'H'm?'

'Oh well, if I'm boring you!' Davina turned over crossly, presenting her back to him, but instantly his hands pulled her against him, sliding round to cup her breasts as he fitted against her so that she lay in the angle of his body, while his lips roved over the nape of her neck. His fingers teased her nipples until her breath rattled in her chest, and she couldn't help pushing herself against the stirring hardness thrusting against the back of her thighs. Suddenly Leo turned her to him and she cried out even as her body accommodated the thrust of his.

Davina lay for a long time afterwards in complete silence, her head buried in her pillow, her back turned to Leo.

'Did I hurt you?' he asked eventually.

'No.'

'Are you angry with me?'

'No.'

'Then what's the matter?'

'I would have thought that was obvious.' Davina trailed into silence, scowling in the darkness.

Leo turned her gently towards him. 'If you didn't like it I'll try to restrain myself in future.'

'But that's just it!' she blurted. 'I did. When we were in the middle of having a row! Am I supposed to?'

He shook with laughter. 'Surely you aren't shocked?'

'Stop laughing at me!'

'Oh Davy. You're delicious!' And he stifled her protests with kisses until she gave up and settled down happily for sleep in his arms, all thoughts of Madeleine utterly routed from her mind.

CHAPTER TEN

WHEN Madeleine Lennox finally put in an appearance Davina was waiting alone at Ty Mawr to welcome her. The rest of the unit were shooting outdoor scenes with Jack and some of the supporting cast, and no one was about as Davina stood quietly in the portico of the house as the tall, slender figure emerged from the taxi.

'Hello, Madeleine,' said Davina, and held out her hand.

Madeleine Lennox was several years older than Davina, but she looked young and awkward in her uncertainty, her heart-shaped face in its frame of cloudy dark hair pale and strained as she took the outstretched hand.

'Hello, Davina.' Her eyes dropped to Davina's other hand, to the new wedding ring and the half-hoop of rubies and diamonds. 'It was such a surprise when your mother told me—because it was Leo, I mean. Oh, God, this is difficult! Anyway, sincere congratulations.'

'I know it's awkward,' said Davina cheerfully. 'But we can't pretend you and Leo weren't lovers once, so we must just make the best of it.'

Painful colour rose in Madeleine's face. 'I don't suppose he's very thrilled to have me in his film, is he?'

Davina led the way indoors. 'He wasn't at first. But the professional in him's pleased with the idea now. You're so perfect for the part.'

'Neurotic and unstable, you mean.' Madeleine smiled ruefully.

'No. Beautiful and a very good actress! Now let's have

some tea before the rest of the crowd get back.'

After two cups of tea and some feather-light scones Madeleine looked better. 'Even so, I can't say I'm looking forward to meeting Leo one bit,' she sighed.

'But you've met occasionally over the years, he told me.'

'Oh, yes. But, goodness, Davina, this is really your honeymoon, such as it is! Not the best time for me to be hanging around.'

There was a constrained little silence, then Davina suddenly asked, 'How long were you and Leo together, Madeleine?' The words were out before she could stop them, and she cursed herself silently.

Madeleine bit her lip, and turned away. 'Not very long at all, really. It was over a fair period of time, I suppose, but we were away from each other a lot because we were working on different things. And even though we were both involved in the Byron film with Jack we had to keep our—our relationship quiet because Jack and I were supposed to be having an affair, according to publicity.' She gave Davina a very straight look. 'We never actually set up house together, you know.'

'No, I didn't know,' said Davina thoughtfully. 'The way Leo behaved at the time I just assumed you did.'

Madeleine hesitated for a moment, then took in a deep breath. 'You probably won't want it, but I'd give you one piece of advice, Davy. Don't ever make him jealous if you can avoid it. Leo's a lovely man, but very possessive.'

Davina shrugged cheerfully. 'He's older and wiser now than when you knew him, Madeleine.' And not likely to react so violently over me, she thought privately, and felt depressed. She looked up quickly at the sound of approaching male voices. 'Return of the thespians, I think.'

'I'm not looking forward to this,' said Madeleine, and started up nervously.

Davina was equally tense, filled with sudden dread at the thought of Leo's face when he first set eyes on Madeleine. For all his reassurances, the memory of his berserk rage when Madeleine had run away from him all those years ago was still very fresh in her mind.

But when Leo and Jack came into the room still arguing over some point, Leo's face lit up at the sight of his wife and he took her in his arms, kissing her very thoroughly before turning to Madeleine with a friendly smile. 'So you've arrived safely, then, Madeleine. Good. Now we can get on. You're familiar with the script?'

Madeleine greeted him quietly, held out her hand to John Wynne Jones, then began discussing rehearsals and other technical necessities with Leo, who was so matter-of-fact about the whole thing Jack drew Davina aside, bored, and begged any tea she might have left.

'Marvellous, isn't he?' he said in an undertone. 'Cool as a blessed cucumber. Never think he was ready to commit murder over her once, would you?'

'No,' admitted Davina, striving for objectivity. 'You wouldn't.'

'Wouldn't what?' asked Leo quickly, coming back to put his arm round her waist.

'Think you and Madeleine were—old friends,' said Jack bluntly, and Madeleine blenched.

'We weren't "old friends" for very long,' said Leo, and scowled at the actor. 'Tactful swine, aren't you?'

Davina let out a nervous giggle, and Jack snorted with laughter, and suddenly all four of them were laughing together, until Paul Delaney arrived to greet Madeleine, curious to hear the joke.

'Sort of *family* joke,' said Jack, convulsed, and Paul shook his head and took Madeleine off to buy her a drink before dinner.

Alone in their room later, Leo and Davina stared at each other ruefully, then Leo sank down on the bed, shaking his head in wonder. 'Now that was rather odd, wasn't it?'

Davina nodded. 'There I was, all keyed up for emotional fireworks——'

'And all you got was a damp squib. Talk about anti-climax!'

'And poor Madeleine really had the jitters about facing you.'

'While Jack, would you believe, had the bloody effrontery to remind me that *you* were my concern now, and I wasn't to hurt you.' Leo's eyes flashed. 'As if I needed anyone to tell me that.' His face went blank 'But where did all my big tragedy go, darling? Now it seems like a storm in a teacup.' He held out his hand. 'Come here and comfort me.'

'If "comfort" is the euphemism I think it is, no chance. I have no intention of being late for dinner again tonight, so go and have a bath.'

'On my own?'

'On your own!'

'I shall expect some form of restitution later,' Leo warned her darkly as he took off his shirt. 'I've had a long, hard day, I'd have you know.'

'Then I suggest an early night.'

'I was hoping you'd say that!'

The days flew by after that, and the weeks with them, once the last trace of cloud had lifted from Davina's horizon. She loved being part of the excitement of making the film, loved sharing Leo's triumph when a scene was played to his satisfaction. It was also a revelation to watch Madeleine Deane the actress, who was a very different being from her off-the-set persona. She was utterly brilliant in her role, as was Jack, and shooting went ahead at a tremendous pace because of the rapport between them, pleasing Leo with the way things were turning out.

'Jack's scenes are actually finished on this section—a fair bit ahead of schedule, by some miracle.' Leo was strolling with Davina in the garden after dinner one night a few weeks later. 'Another day or so with Madeleine on the bit she does with her father and we can move into the studio for the trial scenes.'

'I shall miss this place,' said Davina wistfully. 'I only wish I could have done more exploring with you.'

Leo leaned against a tree and drew her close. 'Not much of a honeymoon for you, was it, my sweet?'

'I've had a wonderful time,' she protested. 'I love being involved with all the filming and watching you at work. Will I be able to come to the studio too?'

'Of course!' Leo shook her gently. 'I married you in a rush because I wanted you with me all the time. I haven't changed my mind. Goose!' He kissed her swiftly. 'Is it too early to go to bed?'

'Yes.'

'Shall we go just the same?'

Laughing, they stole upstairs, trying to avoid the others, not that Leo cared who saw them. 'Not a man in the place wouldn't change places with me, I assure you, my poppet.'

'Don't call me that. And you're exaggerating about the others.'

'Not a bit of it. In fact Jack's been pestering me to let him take you on a climb up Mynydd Mawr over there tomorrow.' Leo pointed out of the window. 'I refused point blank, but I suppose I'm being selfish. I don't relish the thought of handing you over to Jack for the day, to be candid, but on the other hand it would be a break for you. Would you like to go, love?'

Davina looked at him steadily. 'Would *you* like me to go, Leo? Just say so if you don't. I'm not all that keen.'

Leo kissed her gently. 'It would do you good. You look a bit pale and heavy-eyed, Davy. Since I've been working you haven't had much good Welsh air. Spend the day with Jack. You'll enjoy it.'

Davina giggled. 'Especially if I keep reminding myself how many females would give their eye-teeth to be in my shoes—or climbing-boots in this instance.'

Leo shook her. 'Just remember you're a respectable married lady.'

She laughed, and reached up to kiss him. 'So remind me, husband—as only you know how!'

The following morning Davina was up before Leo to find the weather was sunny and crisply cool, the view from the windows even more spectacular now the leaves were turning colour to gild the landscape. Jack was waiting for her downstairs, looking unusually work-manlike in heavy sweater, moleskin breeches, thick socks and climbing boots, a rucksack on his back.

'Aunt Del made us some lunch,' he said briskly, 'so come on then, young Davy—for God's sake tear yourself away from that man of yours and let's get cracking.'

Leo went outside with them, giving a stream of instructions to Jack on taking care of Davina, seeing she didn't get tired, bringing her back early, until the actor turned on him and told him to run away and direct his film and let them get on in peace.

'That husband of yours is like a hen with one chick where you're concerned,' grumbled Jack as they left the hotel.

'Nonsense.' Davina dismissed the idea airily. 'He used to know me when I was young, that's all. Still thinks I'm seventeen sometimes.'

'He's potty about you, girl! Never takes his eyes off you. Talk about besotted bridegrooms——'

'Oh, shut up, Jack.' Davina coloured. 'Leo may have been like that Madeleine, but it's different with me.'

Jack's handsome face wore a sceptical look as he let her through a five-barred gate and closed it carefully behind them. 'You could have fooled me, *cariad!*'

Davina changed the subject, telling him she wanted to concentrate on the climb, which was undemanding at first, and led upwards gradually via a farm track with cattle-grids at regular intervals. The air was cold and pure and the sun shone from a cloudless sky as they kept up a brisk pace, while Jack gave her a description of his childhood in the village they could see below them in the distance. Davina had never been in this part of Wales before and was deeply impressed by the grandeur of the imposing range of 'hills' as Jack called them, not as remote and awe-inspiring as Snowdonia, but very majestic just the same.

'Can't you just picture Owain Glyndwr up there in one of those clefts,' said Jack, waving an expressive arm, 'lying in wait to sweep down on the invading English.' His eyes glowed beneath his windswept curling hair and Davia listened, fascinated, as he told her tales of local myth and folklore in the celebrated, resonant voice that had made his fortune.

It was very warm by the time they called a halt mid-morning. They perched on some boulders while they drank strong coffee from a flask, and Davina dispensed with her sweater before resuming the journey upwards. Her hair was pulled back from her face in a single braid, and she wore a sweatshirt of Leo's with a pair of dark blue track-suit trousers, a rolled cagoule strapped to her back, and as the track grew steeper Davina found she was beginning to perspire and breathe more heavily, and grimaced at her lack of fitness. Jack, on the other hand, moved as easily as if he were strolling along a city pavement.

'How come you're so hale and hearty?' panted Davina as he turned to give her a hand. 'You look so pale and haggard most of the time. Your fans wouldn't recognise this fitness freak I've got with me today.'

'I spend an hour or so in the cellar at Ty Mawr every night with young Gareth on the Nautilus equipment, and in town I belong to a club where I can swim and pump iron now and again.' He grinned at her. 'Contrary to popular belief, I do not divide my time between nightclubs and assorted feminine beds.'

'How disappointing!' Davina had discovered her second wind by this time and applied herself to the next part of the climb with renewed enthusiasm after Jack told her they were making for a shepherd's hut to eat their lunch. The meat pies and cheese-filled crusty rolls provided by Jack's aunt tasted epicurean after their exertions, and Davina wolfed her share as quickly as Jack, then ate an apple, drank more coffee, and pronounced herself ready to start again.

It was past two when Jack finally hauled Davina up on to the summit of Mynydd Mawr, which flattened out at the top, forming a narrow plateau where they could sit and gaze at the panorama below, at roads like narrow white ribbons looped around the green hills, and the glint of the river on the valley floor.

'Thank you so much for bringing me up here, Jack,' sighed Davina in bliss. 'Think of the rest of them down there in Ty Mawr, closeted in the disused kitchen with all those lights. They must be sweltering.'

Jack wasn't listening. His dark eyes were focused on the sky above the peaks and he scanned the skyline, frowning, and got up, pulling Davina with him. 'Come on, Mrs Seymour, I think we'd better get our skates on, I don't like the look of the weather.'

'But it's beautiful, Jack,' she protested as she followed him to the edge of the plateau.

'There's a suspicious look about the sky to the west, my lovely. See?' He pointed at a thick border of grey edging the brilliant blue.

'Rain?'

'Mist, more likely. Whatever it is we don't want to get stuck on Mynydd Mawr in it.'

They wasted no more breath on conversation after that as they concentrated on the descent, which was relatively easy, with no need for ropes at any stage, and with plenty of hand and foot-holds on the more difficult parts. Even so, Davina found she had less enthusiasm for climbing down than climbing up. Also, although he encouraged her from time to time, Davina could tell Jack was anxious to get her down this most difficult part as quickly as possible, and helped her as much as he could. His long legs would have covered the scree-strewn slopes much more rapidly on his own, she knew, and she did her best to make as good time as possible, particularly since the insidious band of grey was encroaching fast, blotting out the earlier blue brilliance and obscuring all but the nearest peaks. Soon it was like looking down on cotton wool as they neared the hut where Jack had left the remains of their picnic.

'Good,' said Jack tersely. 'A swig of hot coffee will do us the world of good, *cariad,* though no hanging about, mind. We must get on.'

Davina would have sold her soul for a rest for a few minutes by this time, but stumbled down the track towards the hut after Jack, hardly able to believe her eyes when he leapt down over an outcrop of rock and missed his footing, crashing to the ground and rolling over and over down the slope until his head came into sickening contact with a boulder and he lay still. Horrified, Davina scrambled down after him as quickly as she could until she could drop on her knees beside him. He was unconscious, with blood oozing from a contusion on his forehead, and he was deathly pale. Automatically she felt for his pulse and breathed more easily. It was a little rapid, but not too bad, and she sat back on her heels, staring with dismay at the blanketing mist, which obscured everything except for the shape of the hut a few feet away.

Suddenly Jack groaned and tried to sit up and Davina helped him, supporting him while his head cleared.

'What happened, Davy?' Wincing, he touched a hand to his forehead, then cursed as he saw blood on his fingers.

'You fell and hit a rock. Now, if you could manage to stand up, perhaps we could at least get to the hut, Jack.'

Groaning, he got to his feet with her help, staggering as he stood upright. Davina put his arm along her shoulders and half supported, half dragged him to the hut, where he sat heavily on the bench lining one wall, breathing hard.

'Bloody stupid thing to do, Davy. Very sorry. Feel sick——'

He lunged for the door and she helped him, hanging on to him while he parted with his lunch, then she installed him on the hard seat again, wiping his forehead with her handkerchief.

'Feel better, Jack?'

'A bit. God—sorry about that.'

'Don't be silly. I'm a nurse, remember. Now, let me

see that cut.'

Jack's rucksack boasted a small first-aid kit, to her relief, and Davina quickly swabbed his wound with disinfectant, then taped a dressing over it and took stock of their assets.

'Half a flask of coffee, two apples, some chocolate biscuits—not bad, Jack.'

He sat with his head against the wall, his face ghastly in the gathering gloom. 'There's a shelf in the corner, Davy. Probably some candles on it. I've got some matches.' He peered at his watch. 'Only four. Blast. Until they knock off at six or so, no one's even going to miss us.'

Davina had worked this out for herself long since. 'Perhaps you'll feel better soon.' She stood on tiptoe to explore the shelf. 'Yes—two candles *and* some matches. Maybe later we can start down if you feel up to it.'

'Even if I did—which I don't at the moment—we're not going anywhere in this. One foot wrong and over we'd go. It's a long way down in some places, love. I'm afraid we'll have to stay put until it lifts. If it lifts.'

Davina's heart plummeted as she pictured Leo's reaction when she failed to put in an appearance. Her professional instincts were troubling her, too. By the light of the flickering candle Jack looked very unwell, and he was shivering. She was cold herself by this time, amazed that the beautiful day had undergone such a drastic change so suddenly. They each had a thick sweater, a waterproof cagoule, and Jack's rucksack also contained a groundsheet which Davina spread on the dirt floor, then she put on her sweater and drew Jack down on the floor beside her, putting their cagoules over them as a gesture towards covering.

'Right,' she said matter-of-factly. 'Now we huddle together for warmth, John Wynne Jones.'

He managed a ghost of a chuckle and obediently put his arms round her, his teeth chattering. 'And you a respectable married lady, too, Davy!'

'I happen to be very chilly as well as married, and you're suffering a bit from shock I think, so let's try and keep each other warm. Do you still feel sick?'

'No, *cariad*. Just very ashamed of myself for getting you into this mess. But the forecast never mentioned fog for these parts, I swear it.'

'Perhaps the sun's shining down on Ty Mawr at this very moment.' Davina shivered and burrowed closer to him, holding him close, and Jack obediently tightened his hold on her small body. 'If we stay as still as we possibly can we'll conserve our body heat,' she said briskly, and felt Jack shake against her.

'Yes, nurse,' he said meekly.

Davina was right. After a while Jack stopped shivering, and their body contact began to generate enough warmth to make their vigil marginally bearable. They talked about everything they could think of. Jack recited all the Shakespearean verse he could remember, which was considerable, then Davina recalled all the funny bits from her hospital training days until after an hour or so she decided they could treat themselves to the last of the coffee. Afterwards, tightly clasped together again, they did they best to keep cheerful, but conversation lapsed frequently, and Davina worried when she detected sounds of strain in Jack's voice, though he swore he was all right. The luminous figures on his watch showed a few minutes past seven when Davina got up to check the fog, but a solid white wall met her eyes outside the hut and she swallowed hard, trying not to panic over Leo and how frantic he must be. When she turned she found Jack on his feet, swaying groggily as he peered at the weather.

'As you were, Jack,' she ordered. 'Fog or no fog, you're in no fit state to climb down a mountain. And I, for one, have no intention of carrying you down.'

'How disobliging,' he said, aggrieved, but sank down wearily on the floor as Davina arranged their inadequate covers over them and they resumed their former positions.

'Our best bet would be to get some sleep,' she said.

'We can try,' said Jack in an odd voice.

'So close your eyes and relax!'

A smothered snort was her only answer as she followed her own instructions and closed her eyes, snuggling up to the thick wool covering Jack's chest, trying to imagine it was Leo who was holding her. The events of the day had taken their toll, and to her surprise she actually did feel drowsy, despite the hard floor and the cold, and dozed a little, but disturbing fragmentary dreams troubled her sleep and she woke with a cry to the sound of Jack's deep, soothing voice, and the touch of his cheek against hers. An involuntary sob shook her as she realised where she was, and Jack's arms tightened. 'Don't cry, *cariad,* please! You've been such a brick—it won't be long now,' and with a groan he kissed her before she had time to realise his intention. Davina struggled to push him away and suddenly there were shouts and noise and light shining in her eyes.

'What the hell are you two playing at?' grated an incensed voice, and Davina sat up with a jerk, disentangling herself from Jack as the hut seemed all at once full of men and torches, and Leo, who yanked her to her feet with a heave that threatened to dislocate her shoulder.

'Jack fell down and broke his crown,' said Jack groggily, staggering to his feet. 'Hey, steady on, Leo. The poor girl——'

'You bloody well stay out of it, Jack,' snapped Leo, eyes blazing.

'What the hell——'

'Leo,' interrupted Davina, suddenly angry herself, and not in the least self-conscious in front of Owen Wynne Jones and Gareth, and someone else behind them, whom she couldn't see in the dim light. 'The mist came down and we couldn't see, and Jack fell and hurt his head.'

'If he was so badly injured would you mind telling me what you were doing rolling about on the floor together?' demanded Leo in fury.

'Look here,' said Jack hotly, lunging forward, but his uncle intervened promptly, pulling him away.

'I imagine it was to keep warm,' he said hastily. 'My wife tells me you're a nurse, Mrs Seymour, so I'm sure you coped very well.'

'I tried,' she said dully. 'I thought we'd do better if we stayed close for warmth.' She met her husband's accusing eyes. 'No strawberry-embroidered handker-chief, Leo?'

No one else picked up the allusion, but Jack's eyes flashed. 'Oh I see. Cast as Cassio, am I, Leo? You'd do better to stick to directing than hamming it up as Othello. Anyway, you're off your head.' He swayed a little, and Gareth put out a hand to steady him as his father took over firmly and guided his nephew out into the thinning mist. The man in the background moved forward and spoke quietly for the first time.

'Come on, Davy. Let's stick with the others—no point in getting lost a second time.'

'Sean?' Davina stared up at her brother, stunned. 'What are you doing here?'

'Helping Leo look for you.'

The return journey down the mountain was relatively

swift, but otherwise ranked for Davina as one of the least pleasant experiences of her life. They kept up with the others as instructed, Davina stumbling along between her husband and her brother, neither of whom addressed a single word to her personally. They exchanged brief snatches of conversation above her head from time to time, about the film, about Sean's latest mission, each of them holding her by an elbow as if she were a piece of luggage they were intent on getting back to the hotel at top speed. Davina could sense the anger in Leo, the vibrations reaching her clearly, as though he were hitting her, but she felt too exhausted to do anything about it. She couldn't even be bothered to ask about Sean's unexpected appearance, due to the aches and pains which were beginning to make themselves felt all over her body. They intensified, and she began to feel vaguely sick, then told herself firmly she had no reason to feel sick. Jack was the one who had hit his head. Again. She chuckled feverishly. Perhaps he'd bumped the same place as before.

'Is something amusing you?' asked Leo icily.

'Not really.' Suddenly she dug her heels in. 'I'm going to have to stop a moment.'

'For crying out loud, Davy,' said Sean impatiently. 'Let's get back to the hotel. Madeleine's off her head with worry about you.'

And heaven forfend that we worry Madeleine, thought Davina nastily, then tore herself away from her captors to be mortifyingly sick. They stood aside, looking helpless, she noted with a glimmer of amusement when she turned back to them.

'You're cold,' said Leo grimly, and took off his leather jacket to put it round her shoulders. 'Why didn't you say you felt sick?'

Davina ignored him, absorbed by her aches and pains

again as they reached Leo's car, which was waiting as far up the track as he had been able to drive it.

'Where's Jack?' she asked feebly.

Leo breathed in sharply. 'In Owen's Land Rover. Come on—just a few more yards.'

But the grinding ache had gathered itself together and centred in one particular place and Davina gasped and stood still.

'Will you come *on,* Davy,' said Sean irritably.

'Sorry——' she got out. 'Can't——'

With a curse Leo picked her up, throwing the keys at Sean. 'You drive.' He laid Davina on the back seat and got in beside her, taking her ice-cold hand in his. 'What's wrong, Davy?'

She tried to tell him, but the words wouldn't come. She let herself sink into the sick waves of pain, too tired to try to fight them any more. It was so much easier just to go under, to escape from Leo's fury; from everything.

Davina woke to bright lights and a very familiar smell of heat and rubber and antiseptic, and found she was flat on her back on a trolley someone was negotiating through the door of a small hospital room. Minutes later, settled in the bed by the light of a discreetly shaded lamp, Davina looked listlessly at the brisk retreating form of the nurse and saw Leo hovering in the doorway.

'Ten minutes, Mr Seymour,' said the nurse. 'Mrs Seymour needs rest.'

Leo moved to the side of the bed and stood looking down at Davina. He looked tired and remote, his face colourless underneath hair that flamed in the light from the lamp.

'How do you feel?' His voice sounded unutterably weary. Rather similar to the way she felt, thought

Davina. Only she felt sore and depressed and unappetising as well.

'A bit tired.'

'Not surprising.'

'No.'

They looked at each other in silence, then Davina turned her head, wishing he would go. She wanted her husband as he'd been before, sexy and demanding, even if he wasn't in love with her. She could handle that, as long as he wanted her, liked being with her. This distant stranger wasn't Leo. Not the Leo who had held her in his arms and made love to her. This man didn't look as if he had ever made love to anyone.

'There was no time to bring you anything,' he said.

'I don't need anything. I shan't be here long.'

Silence again. Then Leo said abruptly,

'How the hell could you climb up there, Davina, knowing you were pregnant——'

'I didn't know.'

His voice was scathing. 'You're a nurse, for God's sake!'

'So you keep reminding me.' Davina looked away. 'My—my system's always been erratic. It honestly never occurred to me. Not until I aborted, anyway.'

'Aborted!' Leo sounded sick.

She turned to look at him. 'Medical term. Old habits die hard.'

The nurse popped her head round the door. 'Time, Mr Seymour.'

He smiled at her faintly. 'Just a moment or two, please.'

She whisked out again and Leo turned back to Davina, his eyes questioning. 'Will you tell me one thing, Davina?'

She frowned uneasily. 'What is it?'

'Was the baby mine?'

The words struck Davina like a fusillade of shot. As her face lost what little colour it had Leo moved towards her involuntarily, but she found the will from somewhere to raise her hand. 'No—please! Don't touch me.' Her eyes, dull still from the anaesthetic, lifted to his. 'If you found it necessary to ask, Leo, I see no point in answering. Just—just go.'

He hesitated, his face as white as hers, then the nurse came in and he was forced to leave. 'I'll see you tomorrow,' he said at the door, his eyes holding hers with a look of such intensity she knew he was trying to get something across to her. Too tired and too deep in misery to care what it was she turned her head away as he left, unable to control the tears which dripped down her face on to her pillow, and the nurse exclaimed and gave her brisk comfort, assuring her how natural it was to feel depressed under the circumstances.

Mrs Lennox arrived next morning, in company with Madeleine, both of them deeply concerned. Leo, it appeared, was finishing off shooting the film, Sean was writing a story about it, Jack was in bed, and everyone sent their best wishes to Davina, shocked at her misfortune.

'I'm all right—honestly.' Davina was sitting in a chair by the window in a hospital gown and striped regulation towelling robe. 'A nine-week miscarriage isn't anything to make a fuss about.'

'But you've only been married for eight weeks,' said Mrs Lennox involuntarily.

'How numerate you are, Mother!' Davina smiled mockingly. 'So I jumped the gun a bit. Not unusual, surely?'

Madeleine took her hand, her beautiful face warm with sympathy. 'Leo was very upset last night. He took it very badly. Sean thought I ought to warn you.'

'You're all very pallsy-wallsy suddenly, aren't you?'
Davina looked away out of the window, swallowing
hard. 'Leo wasn't the only one to be upset.'

Madeleine looked distressed. 'Sean told me they
found you in Jack's arms in some hut, and Leo went
berserk.' She hesitated. 'He does tend to be possessive,
Davy. I know I'm the last one to dish out advice, but if
you and Jack——'

'You can't be serious!' Davina could stay calm no
longer. 'We're not all like you, Madeleine, susceptible
to every handsome face that comes along——'

'That's enough, Davina,' rapped Mrs Lennox, as
Madeleine went white to the lips, whereupon Davina
burst into tears and Madeleine threw her arms round her
and they both wept together while Mrs Lennox provided
tissues and tried to mop them up.

'I'm sorry, Madeleine,' said Davina at last. 'I know
Sean's the love of your life—God knows why, when you
could have had Leo.'

Madeleine managed a watery smile. 'You see? All you
want is Leo. All I want is Sean. But I'll always be sorry I
had to hurt Leo so I could have Sean. And anyway,
Davy, Leo couldn't care a tinker's cuss about me any
more. I was just trying to explain what he's like
about—about fidelity. He gets murderous. That's why I
made you cover up for me and Sean all those years ago.
I was terrified of what he'd do to Sean.'

'Davina, what exactly *were* you doing with Jack
Wynne Jones?' interrupted Mrs Lennox.

'Trying not to expire from hypothermia, pure and
simple, Mother. And I do mean pure. Jack doesn't
harbour any lustful feelings for me, I assure you.'

Mrs Lennox met Madeleine's eyes over Davina's head
for a moment, then stood up briskly. 'Right, we'd best

be off. I've had a word with Sister and you can leave this evening when Leo comes to fetch you——'

'Could you come, Mother?' Davina felt panic at the mere thought of facing her husband again.

'No, I couldn't,' said Mrs Lennox firmly. 'Leo was very explicit about fetching you himself after he'd rung the hospital this morning. He says he'll have finished at Ty Mawr by this afternoon, so he's taking you home tomorrow.'

Home? Where was that? wondered Davina after her visitors had gone. Leo's London flat, or Ivy Cottage?

It was the first thing she asked Leo when he arrived, to cover the flare of resentment she experienced at the sight of him.

'I thought Ivy Cottage for the moment,' he said. 'I'm having my place done over. You'll be quieter at the cottage anyway, while you recuperate. How are you today?'

'Better.'

'You don't look it.'

'Thanks.'

He shook his head impatiently. 'You know I didn't mean that. I meant you look fragile.'

'I *feel* fragile.' Davina took the overnight bag he had packed for her. 'If you'll wait in the waiting-room, I'll be with you shortly.'

'Very well.' He eyed her narrowly. 'I think we should talk.'

Davina's eyebrows rose. 'Do you? I rather thought you'd said everything there was to be said last night.'

After which the journey back to Ty Mawr passed in tense silence, and as they drew up outside the house Davina let herself out of the car, unwilling to allow Leo even the small courtesy of helping her out. Inside the hall she was received with gratifying warmth by all the members of the unit, while Jack hung back with Madeleine, looking oddly diffident. Mrs Lennox firmly ordered her daughter to bed and as Davina docilely obeyed Jack intercepted her as she reached the foot of the stairs.

'I'm very sorry, Davy, love. You shouldn't have let me drag you up to the summit. I feel lousy about it.'

She smiled into his handsome, contrite eyes. 'Not your fault, Jack. I should have known better. How's the head?'

'Bloody, but unbowed.' He glanced over her shoulder and pulled a face. 'But I daren't talk to you any more. Here comes your husband. He's convinced we're two-timing him, you know.'

'Are you, Leo?' Davina looked levelly at the tall, menacing figure of her husband. 'Can you really be suspicious of Jack and me?'

'I don't suppose Jack's less of an opportunist than any other man,' retorted Leo curtly.

'He means, darling,' said Jack, 'that if *he* had been lying on the floor with you for hours he would have been less virtuous than me.'

Leo said something short and extremely vulgar to the actor, who went off, grinning, as Davina went up the stairs in front of her husband, hostility in every line of her body. When they reached their room she turned on him.

'I have something to say, and I'd be obliged if you'd pay attention because I'm too tired to keep repeating it. Since you've taken the trouble to ask, yes, the baby was yours. There was no possibility of its being anyone else's.' She held up her hand as Leo made to interrupt. 'And yes, I've been taking my little pills like a good girl since we married, but I hadn't started taking them when we made love the first time. If your ego needs boosting you might care to know that you must have hit the target that very first night.'

'Davina——'

'Let me finish,' she said inexorably. 'The other point I wish to make is that all I was doing with Jack was trying to keep warm. He was injured and cold and I'm a nurse, so I did all I could to help him. Thirdly,' she faltered for a moment, almost daunted by the frozen look on Leo's face, then blurted, 'I can't understand why you're so jealous about *me*, Leo. Madeleine yes. *She* was your first love, the one you expended all your dreams on. I'm different. I'm not perfectly sure *why* you married me, unless you had some cock-eyed notion of paying back Sean by making his sister fall in love with you. Or perhaps it was simply because I showed such unbridled enthusiasm for your body. Anyway, I can handle the fact that you're not head over heels in love with me, but not your insult about the baby—nor your inexplicable jealousy. So I'm going back home without you, Leo Seymour. I don't think I can take being married to you after all.'

Leo went deathly pale and moved towards her holding out his arms, but let them drop as she eyed them stonily. 'You mean you want a divorce, Davina?'

She turned her back on him. 'I suppose so. But I'm in no hurry. Unless you are, of course.'

'No. Strange as it may seem, it's not exactly flattering to have one's bride run off before the print's dry on the marriage-lines.' His voice was bitter. 'Since I've experienced something very similar before, I'd be grateful if you'd be good enough to wait a little before broadcasting the news that you're leaving me. My skin isn't as thick as it seems.'

'Fine. In that case I suggest you drive me home in the morning, then no one will be any the wiser.' Davina turned round to face him, her eyes glittering with unshed tears. 'But you can sleep on the sofa over there tonight, Leo. I don't think I can face sharing a bed with you.'

There was silence for a moment, while they faced each other through a barrier of hostility as tangible as a screen of glass. Leo's bone-structure looked even sharper than usual as he stood with his hands in his pockets, his brooding eyes locked with hers. It was a toss-up which of them looked worse, thought Davina dully. Leo looked ill and strained, and something more she couldn't quite define. At last he shrugged and turned away.

'Of course. I'll go back downstairs and have a drink. I'll try not to disturb you when I come up.'

Did he honestly imagine she was going to sleep? Davina was consumed by the desire to lash out, to wound, to exact revenge for those four little words of Leo's that had cut the heart out of her. 'Sean will keep you company, I expect. Extraordinary how all three of you are in each other's pockets again.'

Leo paused at the door, his face carefully schooled to blank indifference. 'As I said to you the other night, suddenly all the enmity seemed so unimportant. Not worth all the angst.'

'How strikingly different from your attitude when you first turned up at Ivy Cottage. I got the impression you still felt pretty bitter about it—and blamed me for my part in it, what's more.' Davina's eyes were scornful.

'I've had reason to change since then,' he said without emotion. 'I'll let you get some rest. Go to bed, Davina. You look exhausted.'

After he had gone Davina sat down abruptly on the bed, feeling like a rag doll, limp and spent and desperately unhappy. After a while she roused herself to take off her clothes and crawl into bed, then lay there in the dark, miserable and tense, waiting for Leo to come back. When he eventually came quietly into the room he undressed in the bathroom, then settled himself on the sofa, and Davina had to fight with herself to keep quiet, to avoid pleading with him to come to bed and take her in his arms and comfort her, tell her a divorce was out of the question. For ever and ever we said, she remembered in anguish. And now it was over. She had lost the baby, lost Leo, and at the thought turned on her stomach, her face buried deep in the pillow so that he wouldn't know she was weeping.

In the morning Leo had left the room by the time she woke. A tap on the door brought her upright in the bed, tense and expectant. When her mother came in, carrying a tray, Davina lay back against the pillows, deflated, doing her best to smile.

'Good morning, darling,' said Mrs Lennox briskly, and deposited the tray by the bed. 'Mrs Wynne Jones is short-staffed this morning so I volunteered to bring your breakfast. It's a bit frantic downstairs with all the film people in a hurry to be off.' She stood back, eyeing her daughter. 'How do you feel, Davina?'

'A bit low, but I'm all right.' Davina eyed the tray without enthusiasm. 'I'm not sure I can eat anything——'

'Of course you can!'

It was easier to dispose of the orange juice and a slice of toast than to argue, and Davina lay back eventually, feeling slightly better once she had drunk her coffee.

'Leo tells me you're both going to Ivy Cottage today. Will you be all right?' Mrs Lennox looked worried.

'If I find I'm not I'll send for you,' promised Davina. 'Now I'd better get a move on. Perhaps you'll help me pack.'

Half an hour later Davina was ready to leave when Leo arrived to collect her. Since her mother was in the room Davina suffered his kiss on her stiff, cold lips, then did as he asked and went downstairs to say her goodbyes. Most people had gone already, and only Sean, Madeleine, Paul Delaney and Jack were there in the hall when she went down. She smiled in response to their queries and went to thank the Wynne Joneses for their kindness, then, all too soon for her own peace of mind she was alone in the car with Leo and they had left Ty Mawr behind. Davina looked back at the house as the car went down the driveway, her eyes heavy. She had been so happy there during the weeks of her odd, working honeymoon. Not merely her honeymoon, she realised suddenly, stricken. Her entire marriage had been spent at Ty Mawr.

The journey back was silent, apart from an occasional query from Leo as to her well-being, or a remark about the traffic or the weather, which was dull and grey, like Davina's mood. She was profoundly relieved when they finally arrived at Ivy Cottage, which was wonderfully warm, bright with flowers, and shone as though it had been newly spring-cleaned.

'Lovely,' said Davina. 'How——?'

'I sent a key to your friend Helen Bates,' said Leo, bringing in the cases. 'I asked her to organise things for you. Where shall I put your bags?'

'In my bedroom, please,' said Davina, her face shuttered, and went to the kitchen, her eyes misting as she saw an unfamiliar casserole sitting on the counter with 'Welcome Home' printed in large letters on the card propped against it. 'Helen's been very busy,' she called over her shoulder, and filled the kettle. 'Want some coffee?'

'I'll make it,' said Leo firmly. 'You sit down.'

Davina opened her mouth to argue, then closed it again as she saw Leo's expression, and went back to the parlour to open the letters stacked in a pile on the small table. 'My uncle's sent us a generous cheque——' she began, then stopped. The cheque was a wedding present. What was she supposed to do with it now the marriage was over?

'Put it in your bank account,' said Leo, reading her mind as usual, as he placed a tray beside her.

'That hardly seems right under the circumstances.'

'I think one sends back the presents when the bride has the forethought to cancel the marriage beforehand,' he said evenly, 'not when she changes her mind after the ceremony.'

Davina flinched, but bit back a reply. 'Coffee?' she asked politely.

'No, thanks. I think I'd better be off now, Davina.'

She stared up at him, startled. 'You're leaving *now?* I mean—don't you want dinner?'

Suddenly Leo's rigid self-control disintegrated, and he stood over her, his eyes glittering darkly in his haggard face. 'It will no doubt astonish you to learn, Davina, that the very thought of eating chokes me at this precise moment. So I'm going. There's enough food in the house to last out a siege, all the bills are paid in advance for the next six months, so all you have to do is get well. On your own, of course, as you've so manifestly indicated you prefer. If you feel ill you can ring Helen, or your mother. Do whatever you like. But how you can expect me to stay here under the circumstances is beyond my comprehension.'

Davina jumped to her feet, glaring up at him. *'I'm* the injured party, Leo Seymour, not you. *I'm* the one who should be furious.'

'Really!'

'Yes, really! Also badly hurt, I'd have you know. *You* were the one who doubted the parentge of our child—how do you expect me to behave towards you? You haven't apologised for even thinking such a foul thing.'

'I might remind you that *you* haven't apologised to me for all those hours you spent in Jack Wynne Jones's arms while I went off my head with worry about what had happened to you!' Leo's jaw was clenched tightly and his face paper-white.

Davina's breath left her suddenly and she sat down. 'You mean I'm the one who's in the wrong?'

'No. But I just need you to say you were sorry for that kiss I witnessed with my own eyes; that it was none of your doing, that all you wanted was to get back to me. You never said a word on the way down the mountain by way of explanation.'

Davina looked up at him scornfully. 'How extra-ordinarily remiss of me. You might take into account the fact that I felt a little unwell at the time, that I was trying to cope with the disaster that was about to overtake me. A double disaster, in fact,' she added bitterly. 'Not only the loss of my child, but the utterly unforeseen doubt about its parentage.'

Leo stood with hands clenched at his sides, staring down at her, and Davina held her breath, almost certain he was about to pull her up into his arms. Then he flung away.

'Goodbye, Davina.' His voice was barely recognisable as he went to the door. 'Take care of yourself.'

Some strange instinct for self-destruction forced her to ask, 'How about the divorce?'

Leo paused, his hand on the door-latch, and turned a blank, unwavering stare on her. 'Divorce? Oh no,

Davina. I'm not magnanimous enough to let you go legally.'

'Why not?'

His smile was frigid. 'In my profession it's quite convenient to have a wife in the background. Prevents —complications, you could say. Besides, being tied to me will frustrate any hankerings of yours to run to Jack's arms.'

This couldn't be happening, thought Davina despairingly. 'What makes you think I wouldn't anyway, Leo?'

'Just a hunch.'

Their eyes locked for a few tense moments, then Davina turned away wearily.

'Goodbye, Leo.'

There was no answer from him, and she kept her eyes shut, willing him to leave, until the soft thud of the closing door meant she was alone, at last, with her desolation.

CHAPTER ELEVEN

ON A freezing winter day the following January Davina arrived home from her stint at the practice to find a larger pile of letters on her mat than usual. She picked them up on her way through to the kitchen to switch on the oven, leafing through them idly as she shrugged out of her coat. As usual there were no bills. Her rent, electricity and telephone were taken care of by Leo, who also paid a very generous allowance into her bank account. Davina had seriously considered moving out of the cottage at first, her reaction one of furious repudiation of anything to do with him. But her post as secretary at the practice had been filled, she had no job, and to cap it all the entire world imagined she was happily married to Leo, who came down regularly at weekends to Ivy Cottage, ostensibly to visit his convalescent bride.

Leo's actual motives were less admirable. When, to her utter consternation, he appeared the first weekend unannounced, he informed her coldly that his appearances at the cottage were intended as proof of co-habitation to the outside world, making divorce out of the question should Davina entertain any idea of suing for it herself. From then on the well-known Jaguar stood conspicuously in Glebe Lane from time to time, while inside, in Ivy Cottage, Mr and Mrs Leo Seymour enjoyed tense, uncomfortable weekends in semi-detached isolation, Davina downstairs, Leo upstairs.

Davina was blazingly angry, while at the same time only too aware that both of them were behaving like silly idiots. But nothing on earth could have made her use the communicating door again herself. The first time had resulted in the most unforgettable experience in her life, she conceded, but also in a pregnancy that had ended their marriage before it had properly begun. If anyone were to use that door in future it would have to be Leo, not her. She even went so far as to buy a bolt, and asked Helen's husband to fix it for her, with the excuse that she felt safer during the week when Leo was away.

A few weeks later one of the receptionists left the practice and Davina, primed by Helen, applied for the job, which was full-time, and a godsend. After a long day dealing with the public and its ills, particularly during the winter months when the work-load was heaviest, she was so tired that she could sleep at nights, and life became more bearable. Christmas was a problem solved by Leo's absence in the States on a promotion of *Dangerous to Know,* also by the flu bug which laid Davina low a week or so before, since this ruled out any question of her accompanying him as far as the family was concerned as neatly as though she had engineered her illness herself.

'For the life of me I can't see why you insist on working, Davina,' Mrs Lennox had said impatiently, when the family were gathered at Ben and Hetty's for Christmas. Her disapproval was by no means lessened when Davina said she liked the work, and needed something to occupy her since she saw Leo only at weekends. In Margaret Lennox's opinion a baby was a much better way of passing the time, and she said so, adding that Davina looked terrible. Davina reminded her that flu was not remarkable as an aid to beauty, but promised to take vitamins, eat properly, and work only her normal hours, with no quixotic offers of overtime.

Which was the reason for the savoury casserole heating in the oven, Davina thought with a grin, as she read a long, frivolous letter from Candida. Obedient little Davina was doing what she was told, and looking better, even to her own eyes, probably because the time without Leo had been a relief in some ways. The last envelope she opened was an invitation to the première of *Dangerous to Know* in Leicester Square. One of the royals would be there, and it promised to be a glittering occasion. Davina wondered if her presence would be required as Leo's wife. She had no idea when he was getting back, since their present unnatural relationship stopped short at letters, even though a Christmas present had duly arrived for her to display to the family, a beautiful antique necklace of topazes set in gold. It had won cries of envy from Hetty and Sarah, but prompted a look of affectionate sympathy from Madeleine, who was far more percipient than Davina found comfortable. Mrs Lennox had praised the present, but was blunt about absent husbands at Christmas time, until the happy excitement of her grandchildren had diverted her.

Davina ate her dinner, then stretched out on the sofa with a sigh, glad to enjoy a lazy evening in front of the television. Monday was the busiest day of the week at the practice and she felt fit for nothing more than some undemanding entertainment for an hour before she went to bed with a book. When a knock on the front door interrupted her a little later she sighed, hoping that Helen hadn't decided to pop round for a chat as she sometimes did, kind though her intentions were. Davina went to the door then stared, open-mouthed, at the man outside.

'Jack! Come in, come in. Where have *you* sprung from?'

Grinning all over his spectacularly handsome face

Jack picked her up, kissed her soundly, then set her back on her feet and whisked her into the room, closing the door behind him on the bitterly cold night. 'I'm on my way to Oxford for a few days to see a pal. Thought I'd call in on the little bride. How's Leo?'

'Leo?' Davina turned away. 'Fine, as far as I know. He's still in the States. What'll you have to drink, Jack?'

He took her arm, pulling her round to face him. 'What's wrong, Davy? Leo's not in the States, love—he flew back with me last week.'

Davina stood still, utterly flattened by the news.

'You didn't know,' said Jack gently. He led her over to the sofa, sitting down beside her with his arm around her waist. 'I've suspected something ever since you left Wales. Leo's been different—even throwing fits of temperament on the set. Not his style at all, darling, believe me. Yet he was always so hell-bent on dashing down here to you at weekends, I assumed——' He stopped, eyeing her in remorse. 'I really mucked it up for you that day on the mountain, didn't I? Bloody good thing Leo wasn't alone when he found us. He looked ready to murder me.'

'He's never forgiven me for—oh, I don't even know exactly. Most of all because I was in your arms and—and——'

'I was trying to kiss you,' he said helpfully.

'That too. And of course he was worried for so long before the fog lifted enough for them to search for us.' Davina's voice was dull and flat. Jack's news had quenched all the life in her. She had been so certain Leo would come to see her as soon as he was back.

Jack turned her face to his, his eyes rueful as they met hers. 'His suspicions weren't entirely without foundation, darling.'

Davina's eyes flashed indignantly. 'Oh yes, they were. Dash it all, Jack, it was his idea that I went climbing with you.'

'Mine too, Davy. *You* were above suspicion, but I can't truthfully say I was. Never have been either, from the first time I saw you in your little nightshirt that morning.' He chuckled mirthlessly. 'Funny, really, isn't it? Jack the lad, the one the girls swoon over, covets his neighbour's wife. All that in-depth characterisation of Byron must have affected my balance.'

Davina jumped up, wide-eyed. 'But, Jack——'

He held up his hand. 'Don't worry, Davy, I'm not about to fall on you, or anything gross like that. I just thought you'd like to know—well, if you do come adrift with Leo——' Colour rose in his face. 'What I'm trying to say is that I'm here to fall back on any time you need a—friend.'

'Oh, Jack.' Davina's eyes filled with tears. 'You're so kind. I do appreciate what you're saying, though it's hard to imagine. John Wynne Jones and Davina Lennox would be far-fetched as a pair, you know.'

'Particularly since you're actually Davina Seymour, my lovely.' His beautiful mouth twisted in a grin. 'Which is why it's not on as far as you're concerned. Right?'

Davina nodded, her eyes bright with self-derision. 'Right, Jack. I saw Leo for the first time on my seventeenth birthday, and I've never been able to think of any other man in that way since. God knows I've tried—oh, for heaven's sake let's have a drink. Hang on a minute, there's sure to be something alcoholic up in Leo's room.' She unbolted the connecting door and ran up the stairs, then gave a stifled scream as she reached the top. Jack tore up after her and thrust her aside, his face blank with astonishment at the sight of the sleeping figure in the bed.

'Good God, it's Leo.' He swung round to face Davina, who stood where she was, her hand to her mouth. 'Didn't you have any idea he was here?'

'Of course I didn't.' Davina came to life and ran over to the bed, her eyes scanning her unconscious husband's face. She lifted his wrist to feel his pulse, bent nearer to him, then straightened, her face angry.

'What's the matter? Is he ill?'

'No, he is not.' Davina picked up the half-empty whisky bottle from beside the bed. 'He's dead drunk.'

Jack smothered a laugh, then drew Davina away. 'Come downstairs before you do him an injury. You look like Lizzie Borden about to wield her axe.'

Whey they reached the parlour Davina shrugged, resigned, at the look on Jack's expressive face. 'OK, OK, you may as well know it all.' She jerked a thumb ceilingwards. '*That's* where Leo spends his weekends. Up there alone, while I'm down here. He doesn't want a divorce, you see—much too convenient to keep a tame little wife in the background. But since I went skipping up Mynydd Mawr with you he doesn't want me either, Jack. Yet he comes down here and parks his car at my door from time to time, for proof of co-habitation, as he puts it.'

Jack leaned against the kitchen counter, his eyes thoughtful. 'He's not happy, you know, Davy. None of the lovely ladies we met in the States lit a flicker of response in him—and Leo's a damned attractive bloke, after all. But he just wasn't playing. I think all he wants is you.'

'Nonsense——' Davina looked at Jack wistfully. 'Do you really think so?'

'Yes, more fool me. And now I'm going before he comes down here and bashes my brains out with that whisky bottle.' He took her by the shoulders and kissed her gently on the forehead. 'So long, *cariad*. See you at the première, if I can find someone gorgeous to take with me.'

Davina scribbled rapidly on a sheet torn from the kitchen memo-pad. She handed it to him with a mischievous grin. 'If you're going to Oxford, look up Candida Mason. Remember her at the wedding?'

Jack laughed and tucked the piece of paper in his pocket. 'The blonde with the navy blue eyes? How could I forget? Is she still unattached?'

'She was when she wrote the letter I got today. If you get a move on she may be even yet.'

Jack laughed as they went to the door. 'Sounds too good to pass up.' His eyes sobered as he looked down at her. 'But I meant what I said, Davy. Just whistle and I'll come. Any time.'

'Thank you, Jack.' she said gravely. 'Goodbye—and drive carefully.'

'So long, *cariad.'* He touched her cheek and went out, and Davina locked up, wondering if she should check on Leo, but decided against it. If he couldn't even be bothered to announce he was on the premises he could hardly expect her to trouble her head about him. Particularly since he was in a drunken stupor. She shook her hair back angrily, and was searching for her book when the connecting door opened and Leo appeared, looking like death.

'Why good evening, Leo, how very nice to see you,' said Davina caustically.'

'Jack gone?' he asked hoarsely.

Davina's eyes narrowed. 'So we *did* wake you.'

'Yes. But in the circumstances it seemed best to lie low.' He fingered his chin, which was rough with a day's growth of beard.

'Couldn't you have said something? You frightened me out of my wits. I had no idea you were in the house.'

His eyes were sardonic. 'Since my bedroom was the last place I expected to see you, it never occurred to me to warn you I was there. I came this morning, to get over the after-effects of flu. Probably whisky on top of antibiotics was a bad idea. Anyway it put me out for the count. I intended to let you know I was here as soon as you came home, but I just didn't wake up. But next time you—er—entertain a man in my bedroom check it's empty first.'

Davina flushed scarlet with anger. 'I was merely borrowing some whisky to give Jack a drink. He called in on his way to Oxford.'

'Does he often "call in"?'

'This was the first time.'

'I heard what he said as he left.' Leo stared down at his feet. 'Are you going to whistle?'

'If I decide to I'll let you know first.'

Leo looked up, his eyes dull. 'Very civil of you, Davina. I wonder if you'd be kind enough to give me a cup of coffee. I don't seem to have any upstairs.'

'Of course.' Davina waved a hand towards the sofa. 'Sit down. Are you warm enough?'

Leo nodded, letting his head fall back against the sofa cushions. 'Yes. Thank you. I apologise for the dressing-gown and pyjamas. It was too much fag to dress.'

Davina made no comment, privately surprised Leo owned any pyjamas, then asked if he was hungry.

'Please don't bother,' he said politely.

'No bother. There's some chicken casserole left over from my dinner.'

'Then thank you. That would be very nice.'

Davina busied herself in the kitchen, thinking how ridiculous they sounded, like polite strangers. The feeling of unreality persisted as Leo ate, since their conversation consisted of a stilted account of Leo's visit to the States, Davina's recovery from her own bout of flu, Christmas with the Lennoxes.

'Thank you for my present, by the way.' Davina smiled brightly. 'The necklace is very beautiful, but you shouldn't have given me something so expensive.'

'Valuable, not expensive. It was my mother's.'

'Oh. But——'

'You're implying your role as my wife is too temporary for you to accept my mother's jewellery?' His eyes locked with hers.

'I merely wondered why you gave it to me at all, under the circumstances.'

'Perhaps I was trying to ingratiate myself into your good graces, Davina.' His eyes dropped to his coffee-cup.'

She regarded him thoughtfully. 'If so you're on the wrong tack.'

'Gifts are no good then?'

'Useless. Remember the Greeks.'

'So what would I have to do—*if* that were my motive?' he said tonelessly.

'If you don't know, I hardly think there's much point in my telling you.' Davina's voice remained gratifyingly cool, but underneath her thick sweater her heart was knocking against her ribs as she collected his plate. 'And now, if you don't mind, I have to be up early in the morning, so perhaps you'll return upstairs.'

'Of course.' Leo got up at once, looking marginally better than when he had arrived. 'Thank you for the food, Davina.'

'Not at all. Have you finished the complete course of antibiotics?'

'Yes, nurse. Goodnight.' He hesitated in the doorway. 'Shall I see you tomorrow evening?'

Davina flushed, to her annoyance. 'Are you staying that long?'

'Yes, I'm staying.' He smiled at her, and unwillingly she smiled back, then his eyes dropped to the bolt on the door. 'Make sure you secure the door behind me.'

Davina hadn't intended any such thing, but the moment Leo was on the other side of the door she rammed home the bolt ostentatiously, so that he could hear, then went off to wash up and get herself to bed, utterly worn out one way and another.

Next day she was all fingers and thumbs at the practice, and so abstracted several of her colleagues asked whether she was well. Davina assured everyone she was fine and Helen laughed, saying it was her husband's absence that was affecting the poor girl, not the flu bug still lingering in the village. Davina was about to mention that Leo was home, then changed her mind, suddenly sensitive on the subject, and not up to the others' teasing should they learn it was her husband's presence rather than his absence that was troubling her.

'Going somewhere tonight?' asked Helen, as they did the rounds at locking up time.

'No,' said Davina airily. 'I just felt like bucking myself up a bit. This is the dress Mother bought me for Christmas.'

'Nice! That amber shade suits you.' Helen's eyes were envious. 'I look terrible in that colour. Your hair looks gorgeous today, too.'

Davina was pleased to hear it, since she had gone to the trouble of getting up at dawn to wash it. As she parted from Helen the icy north wind half blew her home. And when she turned, gasping, into Glebe Lane Davina realised why Leo's presence the night before had gone unnoticed. His car was missing. Her spirits rose as she saw all the lights were on in Ivy Cottage, both upstairs and down, and she let herself in, taut with sudden anticipation. Leo rose, smiling, from his seat on the sofa in the parlour, which looked very tidy. A great mass of dark red chrysanthemums glowed in the deep window-embrasure, an appetising smell came from the kitchen, and Leo looked so much better he bore little resemblance to the haggard man of the evening before. He wore a dark green cashmere sweater over a white shirt, and some heavy moleskin trousers Davina remembered very well. The stubble was gone, his hair gleamed redly under the light and his eyes had lost their cold and distant look.

'Hello, Davina. Busy day?' He helped her out of her coat and, rather dazed, Davina allowed herself to be settled on the sofa, a drink thrust in her hand, as Leo excused himself to have a look at whatever smelt so good in the kitchen.

'This is all very unexpected.' Davina smiled at him as he came back. 'I've never thought of you as domesticated, somehow, Leo.'

'I'm not, particularly. But I can throw a few bits of meat and vegetables into a pot when I put my mind to it.' He grinned as he sat beside her. 'You've never really lived with me long enough to find out. One can hardly count the time at the hotel, or with me up there and you down here as it has been since.'

So it was safety-catches off. Davina drank her wine slowly, her eyes speculative as they met his.

'Are you setting the scene for some particular purpose, Leo?'

'Yes. I want you to come back to me,' he said simply.

Davina clamped down on the surge of excitement inside her. 'I see.'

'May I ask how you feel about the idea?' He sounded tense.

'I'm not sure. Perhaps I should taste your cooking. It

might influence me.'

Leo's stew was surprisingly good, even if his expertise had stopped short of a pudding. As he pressed her to some of the local cheese Davina smiled inwardly. So everyone knew he was here by now anyway, if he had been to the village shop.

'Why isn't your car here?' she asked. 'Were you intent on keeping your presence secret?'

'No. I just didn't feel up to the drive down. I came by train and taxi.'

'You look much better today.'

'I am better.' He helped himself to more cheese. 'Different altogether, in fact. I felt like death this time yesterday.'

'You looked like it. You could have been a corpse, lying there.'

Leo smiled at her ruefully. 'I'm sorry I frightened you, Davy.'

Davy. That sounded so much better that she decided to eat some cheese after all. They finished the meal amicably, then watched a film, which Leo picked to pieces scene by scene until it came to the inevitable explicit love passage, when he went suddenly quiet. When the film was over he got up abruptly and said goodnight.

Davina's disappointment was intense. 'But it's only just ten, Leo. You don't have to leave now.'

'Oh, but I do, Davy. Give it a little thought after I've gone upstairs and you'll realise why.'

Davina gave it a great deal of thought, for some time after Leo had gone. The evening had been comfortable, relaxed, until the love scene in the film. Then Leo had been different, tense. So had she. Watching the bodies writhing on the screen had made her desperately aware of the man sitting beside her. Memories of their nights together had bathed her body in heat, and she had hoped, expected, that he would turn to her and take her in his arms and everything would be all right again.

Davina sat lost in thought for some time, until the truth became plain at last. She loved her husband desperately and wanted him just the way he was, jealousy included, if that was how it had to be. Madeleine had run from him, and, in essence, so had she. Leo's ego had taken a beating both times. Yet last night, even after hearing Jack's parting words, Leo had kept relatively calm, and tonight had made it perfectly clear he wanted her back again. But it was she who would have to make the first move in the actual game of love, it seemed, as proof that she really wanted him.

Davina went to her bedroom and undressed, thinking how very simple it was. All she had to do was go upstairs and climb into Leo's bed. She took out the blush-pink satin nightgown Madeleine had given her for Christmas, slid it over head, brushed out her hair and eyed herself in the mirror. Not bad at all. Then she took a deep breath and ran on bare feet through the hall and lamp-lit parlour, coming to a sudden halt in the middle of the room as Leo came through the connecting door. His eyes blazed as he saw her.

'I was coming to you——' she began breathlessly, but never finished as he caught her in his arms.

'And I was coming to you, my darling,' he muttered in between kisses. 'I couldn't stand it a second longer.'

Davina clung to him fiercely. 'I don't want a divorce, Leo.'

He held her away from him, trying to look stern. 'Just as well, since I never had any intention of giving you one. Why do you think I kept coming down for those awful weekends? Just so you could never say I'd deserted you, my poppet!'

She closed her eyes, trembling against him as the

familiar, wonderful surge of feeling began to overwhelm her in the way she had missed so much she wanted to cry now they were together again. She felt Leo's lips against her lids, heard his husky murmur.

'Don't cry, sweetheart.'

'What have I to cry for?' Her eyes were incandescent as she smiled up at him. 'Love me now. Please Leo.'

Leo drew back, looking down at her with a tenderness that turned her heart upside down. 'I think I always have loved you, Davy, in some kind of way, ever since you were a cuddly little schoolgirl. When I saw you again at the fête, behind that ridiculous stall, I couldn't believe my eyes. Davy, grown up and utterly lovely, and, whatever I had to do to achieve it, mine. Did you feel the same?'

'Of course I did. I always did. And it was a shocking nuisance, I can tell you, because no one else would ever do——' She broke off. 'Do you really mean it, Leo?'

He held her close, rubbing his cheek against hers. 'Every word, Davy. I know I raised hell about Madeleine, but that was different, and frankly I got over it so quickly I soon realised it was not exactly the *grande passion* I'd imagined. Then I met you again and found what I'd been unconsciously looking for all along. The love of my life.' He raised his head to look at her, his eyes dark with the intensity of his emotion, open wide for once with nothing hidden, everything there for her to see. And it was all for her, Davina realised with sudden, elated assurance.

'Second careless rapture, Leo?' Her eyes danced.

'If it is, it's a damn sight better than the first!' He pulled her close and began to kiss her with a sense of urgency Davina recognised and responded to with joy. After a while he drew away, frowning, as he looked down into her bemused eyes. 'But you said once you'd been in love before, too. That it wasn't an experience you enjoyed.'

'True.' Davina cast down her eyes sorrowfully. 'I fell in love with a man who loved someone else, for my sins.'

'Sweetheart——' He bent to kiss her quivering mouth with sympathy, then drew away as he felt her shake. 'You're laughing!' he accused her, then his eyes cleared and began to dance. 'You mean——'

Davina nodded with mock resignation. 'Yes, Leo Seymour, you were the one I fell in love with so hopelessly. Then I spent seven long years convincing myself I was over it. Until I met you again. At which point I realised there'd never been, nor ever would be, any other man in the world for me.'

Leo buried his head against her neck. 'Oh Davy, I don't deserve you. I can't even promise I'll never hurt you again, never be jealous, because I know myself only too well. But I *will* love you for ever, as I once promised. I've never stopped, in spite of the brutal thing I said.'

'About the baby?' Davina drew back to look into his face.

He nodded, his eyes sombre. 'God, if you knew how much I regretted that. It's haunted me day and night ever since. And the stupidity of it is that I never meant it for a moment. I'd been hurt and I suppose I wanted to hurt back. Can you forgive me, Davy?'

'Yes. As long as you make it up to me.'

Leo's eyes looked deep into Davina's. 'How can I do that, darling?'

A laugh bubbled up inside her, lighting up her eyes like lamps. 'Help me make another baby!'

He laughed in delight and picked her up. 'I thought you were going to ask something difficult! Now, there's just one trivial little point to clear up.'

Davina clasped her hands round his neck in bliss. 'What is it?'

'Your bed or mine, Mrs Seymour?'

Their laughter died away as Leo carried her, kissing her, through the connecting door and up the stairs to the scene of their first rapture together. Not that Davina cared where they were. They were together again, which was the only thing in the world which mattered, for ever and ever. And this time round for ever would last a long, long time.

Harlequin Historicals

Step into a world of pulsing adventure, gripping emotion and lush sensuality with these evocative love stories penned by today's best-selling authors in the highest romantic tradition. Pursuing their passionate dreams against a backdrop of the past's most colorful and dramatic moments, our vibrant heroines and dashing heroes will make history come alive for you.

Watch for two new Harlequin Historicals each month, available wherever Harlequin books are sold. History was never so much fun—you won't want to miss a single moment!

GHIST-1

Harlequin Romance

Coming Next Month

2947 BENEATH WIMMERA SKIES Kerry Allyne
Mallory is tired of her international jet-set modeling career and
wants only to manage the outback ranch where she grew up.
Unfortunately, Bren Dalton, the man with the say-so, doesn't think
Mallory capable of it.

2948 SEND ME NO FLOWERS Katherine Arthur
Samantha has doubts about ghostwriting Mark Westland's memoirs,
despite the elderly actor's charm. And when it brings Blaize
Leighton to her door, determined to keep his mother's name out of
the book, her life becomes suddenly complicated....

2949 THE DIAMOND TRAP Bethany Campbell
A schoolteacher's life is thrown off balance when she chaperones a
young music prodigy to Nashville—and falls for the very man she
came to protect her student from! And what about her fiancé back
home?

2950 YOU CAN LOVE A STRANGER Charlotte Lamb
Late-night radio disc jockey Maddie enjoys her life in the quiet
seaside town—until Zachary Nash, a stranger with an intriguing
velvety voice, involves her in a tangle of emotional relationships
that turn her life upside down!

2951 STRICTLY BUSINESS Leigh Michaels
Gianna West and Blake Whittaker, friends from childhood, now
senior partners in a cosmetics company, have known each other too
long to cherish romantic notions about each other. Or so Gianna
believes—until a glamorous rival causes a change of mind...and
heart.

2952 COLOUR THE SKY RED Annabel Murray
As a writer of horror stories, Teale Munro works very unsocial
hours, and he assumes Briony, as an artist, will understand why he
feels able to offer her only an affair. Except that he badly misjudges
Briony and her feelings....

Available in December wherever paperback books are sold,
or through Harlequin Reader Service:

Harlequin Romance

Enter the world of Romance . . .
Harlequin Romance

Delight in the exotic yet innocent love stories of
Harlequin Romance.

Be whisked away to dazzling international capitals . . . or
quaint European villages.

Experience the joys of falling in love . . . for the first
time, the best time!

Six new titles every month for your reading enjoyment.
Available wherever paperbacks are sold.

Harlequin American Romance

**Romances that go one step farther...
American Romance**

Realistic stories involving people you can relate to and
care about.

Compelling relationships between the mature men and
women of today's world.

Romances that capture the core of genuine emotions
between a man and a woman.

Join us each month for four new titles wherever paperback
books are sold.
Enter the world of American Romance.